"You've really gone above and beyond, Jonathan."

Esther smiled. "You've spoiled me even more than you've spoiled Rebekah."

"I *knew* you thought I spoiled the *bobbel*," he ribbed her.

Now it was her turn to stutter. "*N-neh*, I meant, you shower her with attention."

Jonathan guffawed. "I have been holding her too much. Starting today, Rebekah's going to sit in her high chair for meals."

He put the baby into the chair. She went willingly, at first, but kept reaching out her arms for Jonathan. When she stuck out her bottom lip in disappointment, Jonathan could hardly bear to look at her. Fortunately, Leah picked her up and deposited her on Jonathan's lap.

"She's got me wrapped around her little finger, doesn't she?" Jonathan asked with a sigh.

"I can't blame you—she's awfully *schnuck*," Leah answered. Then she put her hand to the side of her mouth, as if telling the baby a secret. "And I don't blame you, Rebekah—he's awfully kind."

Jonathan realized Leah was only joking, but he felt his chest swell...

An Amish Winter

Vannetta Chapman
and
Carrie Lighte

LOVE INSPIRED
INSPIRATIONAL ROMANCE

LOVE INSPIRED®
INSPIRATIONAL ROMANCE

Recycling programs
for this product may
not exist in your area.

ISBN-13: 978-1-335-48859-6

An Amish Winter

Copyright © 2020 by Harlequin Books S.A.

Stranded in the Snow
Copyright © 2020 by Vannetta Chapman

Caring for the Amish Baby
Copyright © 2020 by Carrie Lighte

This edition published by arrangement with Harlequin Books S.A.

For questions and comments about the quality of this book,
please contact us at CustomerService@Harlequin.com.

Love Inspired
22 Adelaide St. West, 40th Floor
Toronto, Ontario M5H 4E3, Canada
www.Harlequin.com

Printed in U.S.A.

CONTENTS

STRANDED IN THE SNOW

Vannetta Chapman

This book is dedicated to Sarah Sappington.

To every thing there is a season,
and a time to every purpose under the heaven.
—*Ecclesiastes* 3:1

Be at war with your vices,
at peace with your neighbors,
and let every new year find you a better man.
—Benjamin Franklin

Chapter One

Snow fell heavily as Elijah King directed his horse toward the center of Shipshewana. The streets were virtually empty of buggies and cars. Most sensible folks were already tucked in for the night. Elijah had been out on a job on the west side of town. As usual he was late returning home. Since he was a bachelor, that wasn't exactly a problem.

Thirty-two years old and still a bachelor.

That all changes this year.

He'd made a promise to himself that he would start a family in the next twelve months. Since that usually started with choosing a *fraa*, he was determined to keep his eyes open for any eligible woman. Not as easy as one might think. All the women his age were already married, and the ones who were younger than him… Well, he could remember pulling their *kapp* strings in school. He had a hard time thinking of these younger women in a romantic way. He'd teased most of them with frogs. They were *kinner* when he was in his last year of school.

He expected his bride-to-be would be a brand-new acquaintance. New women did move to town occasionally—usually to marry but sometimes because of family situations. Shipshewana itself was a small community located in northern Indiana, but the Plain community was thriving. *Gotte* could send a bride to him from the far reaches of their country. In fact, he was convinced this was the plan the good Lord had for him. All he needed to do was stay alert and be open to fostering a new relationship.

The snow continued to fall fast and heavy.

Boots tossed his head as they turned onto Main Street. The gelding was ready to be home, and Elijah couldn't blame him. "A warm stall and bucket of oats are waiting for you, Boots."

The horse again tossed his head. He had more personality than any buggy horse Elijah had ever owned, and he'd owned a few. He was thinking of that, thinking of the horse and how difficult it had been to train the gelding to the buggy, when a splash of color caught his eye.

He automatically pulled lightly on Boots's reins, slowing the horse.

A woman wearing a blue coat was standing outside the bus station. Snow swirled around her, reminding Elijah of a snow globe his mother kept on her dresser. The stranger stood with her back to him, but he could tell from her bonnet that she was Plain. She seemed to be transfixed by the sight of the bus that was pulling away.

And in that moment, Elijah knew that this was the woman *Gotte* had promised him. It was ridiculous, sure. He hadn't met her, didn't know a thing about her, but the feeling that their meeting was preordained persisted. Perhaps it was because of the way she appeared as if out of a dream.

Of course, she could be married.

Or promised to another.

On the other hand, perhaps he was supposed to rescue her.

He guided Boots to the parking area outside the Davis Mercantile, where the bus dropped off and picked up passengers. The woman turned at the sound of his horse, and Elijah's eyes widened in surprise. She was holding a babe in her arms.

Definitely married, then.

His dream of finding a bride on a snowy January night evaporated.

Still, he'd do the right thing and offer her a ride.

He set the brake on the buggy, assured Boots he wouldn't be long and slipped the horse's reins around the hitching post.

The woman glanced at him, then back toward the bus, which was quickly trundling out of sight.

He hurried over to where she was standing, under the soft lighting of the Mercantile. "Need a ride?"

Instead of answering, she juggled the baby from her right arm to her left. The child looked to be around six months and was sound asleep. As for the woman, she was a real beauty—tall, thin, with prominent cheekbones and lovely brown eyes.

"I'm happy to take you wherever you need to go."

Elijah was pretty good at reading people. It came in handy when you ran your own business. This woman's body language seemed to be at odds with itself. At the same time that her chin rose a fraction of an inch in defiance, a look of desperation came into her eyes.

"I don't accept rides with strangers."

"So you're expecting someone to pick you up?"

"For all I know you could be a kidnapper."

"I'm Amish."

"You could be an Amish kidnapper."

Elijah was tempted to laugh at that, but one look at the woman squelched any such impulse. "*Ya. Ya*, I see what you're saying. But since I'm in a buggy, it wouldn't be much of a getaway. You could jump out, land in the snow and be fine. Then I'd no doubt be arrested. I suspect a police car would have no trouble catching up with me."

"Maybe you ride around looking for women to prey upon."

Elijah's amusement gave way to irritation. "You have a suspicious nature."

"I'm careful." Her gaze darted down to the babe. "I have to be."

Like snowflakes disappearing on fingertips, his irritation melted away. He stepped closer, but not too close. "I can assure you that I mean you no harm. I saw you standing here and the bus leaving. The mercantile is closed, though there is a pay phone on the other side of the building if you need one."

"*Nein.* I don't need a phone." The words were soft, emphatic, and seemed to hold the heartache of a thousand sleepless nights.

"Perhaps you could contact your bishop for me." She cleared her throat, glanced again at the child and then spoke more boldly. "I would appreciate that very much, if you would."

"Sure. I could do that." Elijah turned the collar of his coat up to keep the snow from hitting his neck. Now that he was standing closer, he could see that her coat was quite threadbare, and the child was wrapped in a blanket that had been patched many times.

"Old Eli doesn't have a phone in his house, though there's a phone shack with a message machine he checks regularly. When it's an emergency, we usually just send someone to his place."

"Would you... Would you fetch him for me?"

"I'd be happy to. He's on the other side of town, though. In this weather, it would take an hour for me to get there and him to get back."

When she didn't respond, he added, "You and the babe would be warmer if you'd just get in my buggy and let me take you to his place."

Her eyes widened in alarm, and she clutched the babe even closer.

"Look, miss. I was just driving through town to my place. There's no need for you to be afraid, but if you'd rather, I can take my horse Boots down to the police station and have them ferry you out to the bishop's in a patrol car."

"*Nein*. I'd rather not ride in an *Englisch* police car." She closed her eyes, pulled in a deep breath and glanced toward his buggy. "We would appreciate the ride."

"I'll just get your bags, then."

He figured she must be on a short visit as she had only a large diaper bag, a small suitcase and a purse with the strap angled across her body as if to ward off any potential purse snatchers.

He picked up the two bags and motioned with his head toward the buggy.

Fortunately he'd left the heater on and the warm air

blasted out as soon as he opened the door. He tossed her bags into the back, then turned to help her, but she'd already managed to scramble up with the child. He unwrapped Boots's reins, tossing them up into the buggy, and hurried around to the driver's side.

If Boots was upset about the change in direction, he kept it to himself.

"My name's Elijah…Elijah King."

"Faith."

He noticed she didn't offer her last name or the child's name. She certainly wasn't much of a talker, or maybe she was simply tired.

"Nice snowfall we're having. They say we could receive a couple feet before morning."

"Which is why I'm stranded here."

"You're stranded?" He glanced her way, but could see only her profile as she was staring out the side window. "Where were you headed?"

"Michigan."

"Ah."

"The bus driver said the roads were closed once you crossed the interstate."

"That happens a couple of times a year. The state will get the roads cleared by tomorrow morning or midday at the latest, but until then… I guess it could be quite inconvenient."

She nodded in agreement. The expression on her face said that *inconvenient* didn't begin to cover it.

They rode along without speaking for a few more minutes. When the silence became more than Elijah could stand, he made another attempt at conversation. "You have family in Michigan?"

"How far now to the bishop's?" she responded.

"Only a few more miles. We'll be there in ten minutes."

"And he's… He's a *gut* bishop?"

"Old Eli? *Ya*. Most certainly he is. Not that old either—I think he turned fifty-five last year. We call him Old Eli because there's also a Young Eli and a Too Tall Eli, and then I'm Elijah—never Eli."

"Too tall?"

"Taller than me even." Elijah was used to being teased about his height. At five foot eleven, he'd always been the tallest boy in his class.

The babe began to fuss, and Faith attempted to console her. Elijah wondered if she had any food in that diaper bag, then decided it was none of his business. The bishop would take care of anything she needed.

"What's her name?"

"Why?" Faith's voice rose in alarm.

"Just being friendly is all."

"Oh." Faith's shoulders slumped a little. "I suppose I'm a bit jumpy. Her name is Hannah."

"Let me guess her age. I'm pretty *gut* at this as I have quite the brood of nieces and nephews. I'd say she's eight months, maybe nine."

"Hannah turned a year last week."

"She seems smaller. Must take after your husband, being as you're nearly as tall as me."

Faith didn't answer that. Instead she murmured something in Hannah's ear and kissed her cheek. That image tore at Elijah's heart and reminded him why he'd vowed to change his focus for the year. To have a *fraa* and a *boppli* would make his life complete. Though he'd prefer one more friendly and lighthearted than the woman sitting next to him.

He didn't know her story, certainly wouldn't judge her, but she seemed taciturn, suspicious and gloomy. He couldn't imagine a worse combination.

"Here we are." Elijah pulled into the bishop's lane.

It was close to seven in the evening, and light blazed in nearly every window.

"Your district allows electricity?"

"*Nein.* The bishop has allowed solar power. He has a good-sized panel on the back of the roof that I installed myself. That's what I do—King's Power is the largest solar business in LaGrange County."

He hadn't intended to boast, but it wouldn't have worked anyway. Faith didn't seem the least bit interested in anything he had to say.

Five minutes later, he'd introduced her to the bishop and his wife, and one of the bishop's sons had fetched her bags. Elijah would have liked to have stayed and heard her story, but he couldn't think up an excuse for doing so. Instead he wished her a good night, told Old Eli to call his business phone if he needed anything and stepped back into the night.

As he drove home, he resumed talking to Boots.

"Guess she wasn't The One."

Boots didn't answer. He was showing his full attitude now that Faith was gone—tossing his head and pulling to the wrong side of the road if Elijah let up on the reins at all.

"Being as she must be married and all."

Elijah felt a familiar heaviness settle over his mood. Being alone was hard, and he didn't know how to fix that. He could fix nearly anything on a solar panel, but life choices? Well, it wasn't as if you could go back and choose again.

How could he have been so foolish as to think a potential wife would pop up in the snow, waiting to be rescued.

Ha! He laughed at that image, as it most certainly did not describe Faith. She'd thought he was a kidnapper.

He fought through the cloud of depression. So she wasn't the woman whom he was meant to marry. That didn't diminish his certainty that he would find the one, and this year, too. Hadn't *Gotte* promised him? At least it had seemed like *Gotte*'s voice when he'd woken on the first day of the New Year, nearly despondent and wondering what the point of all his success was if he had no one to share it with.

As sunlight had risen over his west fields that morning, he'd realized that he had no one to blame but himself. He was the one who had put business first—and maybe that was okay for a time. Not anymore. It was long past the point for shifting his priorities.

Then he'd opened his Bible.

He liked to open it to a random spot as he drank his first cup of coffee. That morning he'd opened his Bible to the third chapter of Ecclesiastes.

To every thing there is a season...

A time to be born and a time to die...

A time to love...

It was as if the words had been written directly to him. He saw, clearly, that his priorities should have shifted long ago. Throughout the next few days, he'd become convinced that *Gotte* had spoken to him. He'd practically sent a letter that read,

Dear Elijah,

It's time you had a wife.

No worries, my son. I'll send you one.

He pulled into his own lane, mentally slapping himself on the forehead. When he'd seen Faith standing in the snow, standing there waiting for someone to come along and rescue her, his heart had quickened. He'd been so sure that she was the woman *Gotte* had promised.

She hadn't wasted any time setting him straight on that point.

She'd certainly wanted little to do with him. Not that she was rude. *Nein*, he wouldn't say that. It was only that she was so reserved, as if she needed to keep a wall of protection around herself and Hannah.

He unhitched Boots, stabled the gelding and added the promised oats to his bucket.

Pulling his coat more tightly around himself, he trudged to his back door. Perhaps *Gotte* was teaching him perseverance. He could stand to learn that. He'd never been a particularly patient man, but he could learn. And then *Gotte* would send his wife. He was certain of it.

Faith knew that she would have to be honest with the bishop and his wife. Old Eli and Mary Ann seemed like a kind couple. Their house was filled with *kinner* and *grandkinner*, who seemed to understand the situation called for privacy. The large family settled back down in the sitting room and left them alone in the kitchen. Mary Ann had insisted she spend some private time in their bedroom where Faith had changed Hannah's diaper, nursed her and then slipped on her *doschder*'s only nightgown—a small white flannel thing that a member from their church district had donated. All of Hannah's things were donated. There was nothing wrong with that, but oh, how Faith would love to have one thing that had been sewn or purchased specifically for her daughter.

She picked up her now sleepy child and cradled her in her arms. "We're going to find our way through this—the two of us will. Never worry, Hannah. *Mamm* will take care of you."

And with that promise, Faith squared her shoulders and walked out into the kitchen.

"There's a cradle at the far end of the table." Mary Ann stood at the stove, waiting on the kettle to boil. "Being as she's small, she'll still fit in it. Go ahead and put her there, then sit. You look dead on your feet."

"Danki."

"Mary Ann keeps several extra cradles around the house," Eli explained.

Eli had gray sprinkled throughout his beard, though his hair was still quite brown. Smile lines fanned away from his eyes. Mary Ann was short and round, and the hair that peeped from her *kapp* was completely gray. There was something about her expression— about the way that she looked at Faith and Hannah— that suggested she understood more than Faith had yet explained. No doubt she'd seen much, as the wife of a bishop. How often had the couple had strangers appear at their door in need of help? Probably they'd heard every conceivable story, even one as woeful as Faith's.

She took courage in that. While her life had been difficult the past two years, she wasn't alone. Others had it worse.

"Seems there are always babes visiting." Mary Ann smiled and pushed a mug of hot tea in her hands. "It's herbal, won't keep you awake at all. Are you sure you won't have a bite to eat?"

"*Nein.* I had a sandwich on the bus."

Eli and Mary Ann exchanged a knowing glance, but they didn't call her on the fact that the sandwich was probably her lunch and not her dinner.

Faith sipped the tea, allowing the chamomile to warm her, soothe her. Finally she raised her eyes to the couple who were waiting so patiently.

"I'm in a bit of a jam, and I could use some help."

"People who care about each other take care of one another," Eli said.

Mary Ann added, "It's not a duty. It's a pleasure."

"But you don't even know me."

"Yet, *Gotte* has brought you to our doorstep. We're happy to help. Share what you feel like you can, and take your time. No one is in a hurry here."

The hands on the clock showed it was nearly eight, and Faith realized that the bishop and his wife would be rising sometime between four and five. She'd imposed enough. No need to keep them up later because she was embarrassed.

Setting down her mug, she clasped her hands on the table. "I was headed for Michigan when the bus put me out."

"Because of the snowstorm." Old Eli glanced at the window. "It's still coming down and the weather people are predicting over a foot."

"If you could provide me a place to stay until the buses are running again, I would be grateful."

"Of course we will." Mary Ann reached out and covered Faith's hand with hers. "How could we do any less?"

Mary Ann picked up her knitting—a soft blue yarn that could have been a shawl or a scarf or a blanket. She was just beginning the project, so it was impossible to tell what it might turn out to be—rather like Faith's life at the moment. The thought simultaneously depressed and intrigued her.

As for Mary Ann, she seemed willing to listen and knit and let her husband pick up the threads of the conversation.

Old Eli tapped the old oak table. "We'll contact your husband too, so he won't be worried. I can send one of the *kinner* to the phone shack at first light—or now if you think it necessary."

"No need. My husband passed two years ago."

"I'm sorry to hear that—we can call your family, then. Surely they'll be worried."

Faith met his gaze. This wasn't the time to indulge in embarrassment or cowardice. The moment she'd stepped on that bus, her life had changed, and she needed to be willing to do whatever was necessary to ensure Hannah's best welfare. She knew that being honest with Old Eli wasn't just the right thing to do, it was the most expedient thing to do.

"That's just it. That's why I'm going to Michigan. I don't have any family. Hannah and I…" Why was this so hard? Why did tears sting her eyes every time she tried to speak of it? Not that she'd spoken to anyone about her trials. In Fort Wayne she hadn't been afforded the luxury of friends.

"Hannah and I are alone. We don't have anyone who will be worried about us."

Old Eli was silent as he sat back and studied her,

but Mary Ann tsked and murmured, "We are all family in Christ, my dear."

"No family where you're coming from…"

"Fort Wayne."

"What about where you're going…in Michigan?"

"*Nein.* I answered an advertisement in the *Budget*. A widowed woman in the Mio district was looking for someone who would be willing to live on the property with her and help run a small farm."

Mary Ann and Old Eli exchanged another look. She wondered about that, the way they were able to communicate without words. She hadn't been married to Jonas long enough to develop such a thing, and his parents—well, Gerald rarely bothered to speak to Sara. When he did, it was usually a command that was meant to be heeded immediately.

"Putting aside for a minute just how difficult it might be for you to help run a farm…" Old Eli held up his hand to stop her protests. "Even a small one, I'm sure you've looked at how far it is to Mio. It's another three hundred miles from here, nearly to the Canadian border."

"And it's a small community besides—and cold. The wind and snow that come off Lake Superior can both try a person's soul." Mary Ann raised her eyes from her knitting. "Are you sure that's where you want to go?"

"I'm sure that I don't have any other options."

Old Eli grinned and pushed back from the table. "Then that is where we will begin."

"Begin?"

"We will pray for options, and that *Gotte* reveals them to you quickly."

Thirty minutes later, Faith was tucked into a bed-

room that was barely large enough to hold the twin bed
and cradle. She thought it might be the room of one of
the teenaged girls as there were books stacked in one
of the cubbies—including several Christian romances
from the public library.

Though the room was tiny, she was grateful for it.
The smallness almost felt cozy, and after sitting on the
bus for so long, she welcomed the chance to lie down.

Hannah was fast asleep.

Faith checked Hannah's nappie a final time before
turning out the room's small battery lantern. As she
lay there in the dark under Mary Ann's clean sheets
and hand-sewn quilt, her mind wouldn't quit wrestling
with the trials of the day.

Gerald's haughty coldness as he'd dropped her at the
bus station, wishing her good riddance and proclaiming he hoped never to see her again.

Sara's tears.

The increasing snow and finally the bus driver's
pronouncement that everyone needed to get off the bus
before they reached the Michigan border.

Being the last one on the bus.

Getting out at the deserted station.

And then Elijah.

She almost smiled when she thought of Elijah. The
look on his face when she'd asked if he was a kidnapper... She would have laughed if she hadn't been so
frightened. How did she know what a kidnapper looked
like? She doubted they wore a T-shirt proclaiming their
intentions.

Elijah King struck her as a guy looking for a woman
to rescue.

Well, she didn't need rescuing.

She didn't need a man.

She'd tried that already, and it hadn't worked out so well.

What she needed was a safe place to raise Hannah, and as far as she could tell that place was in far northern Michigan in the little community of Mio. Sure, she understood it would be cold and isolated, but at the moment a place to live mattered much more to her than convenience.

Old Eli might be a *gut* bishop and a wise man, but he was wrong about one thing.

Options.

She knew better than anyone that at this point, she didn't have any.

Chapter Two

The next morning dawned gray and cold. Faith stood at the window staring at the snow that continued to fall creating giant drifts. She didn't need a weather report to tell her she wouldn't be traveling to Mio. She knew it before Old Eli informed his children that they wouldn't be walking to school, which raised a chorus of happy responses. Not that school was canceled. Amish schools were rarely closed for weather, and today would be no exception.

Still his children laughed and grabbed their coats and lunch pails. Apparently a ride in the buggy on a weekday morning was quite the treat.

"The snow is supposed to continue through tomorrow. Looks like you're stuck with us, dear." Mary Ann patted her shoulder, then hurried into the kitchen to finish the breakfast dishes.

Hannah sat on Faith's lap, playing with a plastic yellow duck, trying to fit the toy in her mouth. She managed to chew on the orange beak, then laughed and showed it to Faith.

Faith was so lost in her own misery that she barely

noticed when Mary Ann finished the dishes and left the room. She was startled out of her reverie when the dear woman placed a box next to the kitchen table and sat down across from her. "There might be some things in there that Hannah could use."

"You don't have to do that."

"Actually you're doing me a favor. I've been meaning to go through them since Sara's been out of diapers."

Faith's head jerked up at the name.

"She's my youngest and in the first grade now. I don't expect the Lord will be blessing us with any more." Mary Beth had been pawing through the box, but she stopped when she noticed Faith's expression.

"Is something wrong?" Mary Ann sat back, apparently in no hurry. "You looked suddenly pale—more pale."

"My mother-in-law's name was… Well, it is Sara."

"Ah."

"She isn't a bad woman, only ineffectual."

"Odd way to describe someone."

"It's the kindest way I know." In order to avoid Mary Ann's compassionate stare, Faith pulled the box closer and began pulling out onesies and dresses, stockings and socks, even small shoes.

"I can't take all of this."

"Well, some of those items are already too small, and others are probably much too big. But anything you think your *doschder* can use in the next few months, you should take." She held up a dress with a ripped seam. "Sara was an energetic child. She still is, for that matter. Some of these are going to need mending."

Which was how they spent the next several hours—dividing items into piles, then mending any small tears.

It was one of the most peaceful mornings that Faith could remember. She felt the muscles in her shoulders loosen up, and the cloud of constant anxiety that seemed to hover over her finally began to dissipate. She found it was possible to actually pull in a full breath. Even Hannah seemed to relax in the cheery, warm kitchen. She played with her duck, then nursed and finally fell asleep in the cradle next to the table.

Faith was thinking on those things, of how much your environment could affect your feelings, when there was a knock at the front door.

She assumed whoever it was had come to see Old Eli, since it was he who answered the front door and then escorted their guest into the kitchen.

Elijah King.

Still tall.

Still handsome.

Still looking at her as if she held the answer to some question he'd yet to ask.

"Elijah came by to see if there's anything we need, Mary Ann." Old Eli snagged his coat out of the mudroom. "Wasn't that kind?"

"It was indeed."

"I'm off to visit Widow Lapp."

"Should I fix you an early lunch?"

"*Nein.* The widow's children always insist that I eat with them, and I think she enjoys the company. After that I'll head to town to fetch some supplies that were supposed to come in. Can I pick up anything else up for either of you?"

"*Danki*, no." Faith had precious little cash in her

purse. She couldn't imagine anything she'd need from town that would justify parting with it.

"Actually I have a list." Mary Ann pulled a slip of paper from her pocket, handed it to her husband, then stood on tiptoe and kissed him on the cheek. "Be safe, dear."

"Always, and I'll be back in plenty of time to pick the children up from school." With a smile and a wink, he was gone.

The moment felt oddly intimate. Faith stared down at her lap wondering why seeing two people who obviously loved each other stirred such confusing feelings in her heart. Certainly there were healthy marriages and happy households. Just because she hadn't experienced one didn't mean that they didn't exist. Her marriage with Jonas hadn't been so terrible—only strained and much too short.

Mary Ann poured Elijah a cup of coffee, then suddenly remembered something she needed to attend to upstairs. Which left Faith alone with Elijah. As if they'd hadn't spent enough awkward moments together the night before.

"How's Hannah doing this morning?"

"Gut." They both stared at her *doschder,* who was lying in the cradle, staring up at a teddy bear mobile.

Seeing Elijah, Hannah began waving excitedly.

"Can I pick her up?"

"Sure. *Ya.*"

She was surprised at how confidently he picked up Hannah. Hadn't Mary Ann mentioned he was a bachelor?

"Nieces and nephews," he said to her unasked questions.

"Oh, *ya*. You mentioned that last night."

"I'm surprised you remember a thing I said. You looked exhausted."

"I remember suggesting you might be an Amish kidnapper, and I'm sorry."

To her surprise Elijah laughed at that. He was certainly a good-natured man, or he appeared to be that way. Not that it was any of her business.

"I guess you've heard the buses still aren't running."

"Old Eli told me."

"You'll be another day late."

"I doubt it will matter."

The little farm in Mio wasn't going anywhere, and the old widow she'd corresponded with had been looking for someone for over a year. She'd gone so far as to tell Faith that if she changed her mind she would understand. "Mio's not for everyone," she had written in her last letter. "But come north and we will see if we're a *gut* fit."

"So you have family there?"

"*Nein.* Not family."

"Oh, I just assumed you were going up to…" His voice faded as he tried to figure out her story and failed.

She could have watched him struggle—there was practically an empty thought bubble above his head—but she decided to have mercy on him.

"My husband passed before Hannah was born."

"Oh."

"Living with my in-laws wasn't… Well, it wasn't safe."

Elijah's mouth formed another O, but nothing came out.

"I found a job in Mio that included a place to live. I corresponded with an Amish woman there who has been a widow for some time. She offered me the job. That's where I was headed."

"Mio, Michigan?"

"The same."

"It's nearly to Canada."

"I'm aware."

Elijah stared down at Hannah, then repositioned her on his lap facing away from him, where she could watch Faith. He reached for the toy duck and plopped it into Hannah's hands.

"I went to Mio once—snowmobiling with a cousin of mine who's Mennonite. I've never been so cold in all my life."

"You don't have to lecture me on the weather in Mio."

"I wasn't lecturing."

"It seemed like you were."

"Not lecturing, but you might want to reconsider."

"Oh, really? You know so much about my life after two brief conversations that you know what's best for me and Hannah?"

"I know you don't want to be in Mio. There's a reason it's a small settlement." He began ticking points off on his fingers, while still effortlessly holding Hannah. "Short growing season. Doesn't thaw once it freezes. The Amish there use sleighs instead of buggies. Less than four hundred Amish in all, which if you do the math is ten to twelve families."

"Just stop."

"Stop what?"

"Stop giving reasons I shouldn't go. It's my decision, Elijah. I thank you for your concern, but it's… It's my decision."

Elijah stood, moving Hannah to his shoulder and pacing back and forth.

"Why Mio?"

"Excuse me?"

"Do you need to be a certain distance from your husband's family? Are they looking for you or coming after you?"

"Of course not, though it's none of your business if they were."

He ignored her jab, still pacing with Hannah on his shoulder. She stared at Faith, smiling as she drooled all over Elijah's shirt. The polite thing would have been to offer him a burp cloth, but at the moment she didn't feel very polite. Elijah King seemed to have everything figured out. Surely he could figure out how to handle a drooling baby.

He turned toward her suddenly. "What's wrong with here?"

"Here?"

"You sound like a parrot."

"And you sound like a busybody." She stood and walked over to where he'd frozen in the middle of the kitchen. Pulling Hannah into her arms, she tossed him a clean cloth diaper. "You might want to use that on the shoulder of your shirt. It's fairly drenched."

And with that she sailed from the kitchen, back to her little bedroom, back to some desperately needed peace and quiet.

She told herself it was because she needed to nurse Hannah. In truth she needed to get away from Elijah King's blue eyes that insisted on searching her own.

She wanted to sound confident, but she was far from it. Mio had been the only thing she could find, the only living situation that presented itself. There weren't a lot of Amish businesses looking for a single mother. She refused to indulge the doubts popping up in her mind.

Mio didn't thaw once it froze? How long was that—six months? And what did she know of Lake Superior and Canada and small communities? She knew nothing about any of those things.

She shook her head, as if she could dislodge the doubts Elijah had planted there.

The snow would stop eventually.

She'd board the bus to Mio, and somehow she'd find a way to make a life there for her and Hannah.

As for Elijah, he could stay in Shipshewana with his solar business and his confident answers.

Installing solar panels during a blizzard was virtually impossible, so Elijah spent the afternoon trying to catch up on paperwork. He was a good businessman. His solar panel company had grown so quickly that he'd had to hire two full-time employees, but he wasn't particularly good with paperwork. He stared at the box he used for an in-basket.

Where did all the paper come from?

And what was he supposed to do with it?

He thumbed through the top inch of paper, pulling out any invoices and writing checks to suppliers. He stuffed the checks in the return envelopes, finally located the roll of stamps he'd purchased and affixed one to each bill. Then he bundled up in his coat and hat, gloves and scarf. The walk down the lane to the mailbox should have eased his restlessness, but it didn't.

So instead of going home, he walked next door to his *bruder*'s. No need going in the house; he knew Thomas would be in the barn.

He found him sitting in the barn's small office, oiling a horse halter.

"Thought you'd be here." Elijah flopped into a chair across from the desk.

"Can't be in the fields. Might as well be here doing things I've been neglecting."

Thomas was ten years older and half a foot shorter, and he was beginning to bald. In other words, they looked nothing alike, and their personalities were—likewise—opposite.

Maybe that's what he needed.

A completely different perspective.

So he found himself telling Thomas about finding Faith and Hannah at the bus stop, taking her to Old Eli's, seeing her that morning and learning of her plan to go to Mio.

By the time he'd finished, Thomas had poured two mugs of coffee from the pot he kept on the potbellied stove.

"Sounds like you're quite taken with her."

Elijah had just swallowed a big gulp of the coffee, and he proceeded to choke on it. Thomas apparently found this doubly amusing.

"That's not what I said. Were you even listening?"

"Oh, I was listening to every word you said."

"What's that supposed to mean?"

"It means I can see right through you, *bruder*. You're looking for a wife, for a family. You said as much at dinner the other night."

"I said that I was going to start courting again, once

I found the right woman. Faith Yoder is not the right woman."

"Because she's a widow?"

"Because she's stubborn and doesn't even like me."

"Lots of women are stubborn. I believe Amish women, in particular, are described that way in the encyclopedia. It's not always a bad thing."

Elijah shook his head, pushed away his cup of coffee and rubbed at the headache pulsing at his temples.

"Faith is… She's all wrong for me."

"Is she difficult to look at?"

"What is wrong with you? I'd never pick a wife based on her looks."

"Uh-huh."

"And for your information she's a very nice-looking woman—tall, blond hair that looks like it might curl softly when not hidden under her *kapp* and eyes a lovely brown. I've never seen eyes that could express so much without her saying a word. Too thin, but that's probably from the worry of her situation. She's a fine-looking woman—but not for me."

"That was a lot of detail for a woman you're not interested in."

"Whatever."

"Maybe it's the child you have a problem with."

"Hannah is perfect—soft and sweet and a very well-tempered child from what I could tell." Elijah sat back, his elbows on the arms of the chair and his hands clasped together. "I'll admit when I first saw her, standing in the middle of the snow and the glow of the Mercantile lighting… I wondered if she was The One."

"I knew it!" Thomas dropped the rag he'd been using to rub oil into the halter and played a drumbeat against the table. "She's available, and you didn't grow up with her. Aren't those your two biggest obstacles? Isn't that what you told me less than a week ago?"

"Sure, *ya*. But…"

"Look, if you want her to stay in Shipshe, then you need to find a way for her to do so."

"Find a way?"

"Find her a home and job. Then again, maybe it's not your problem. I'll bet Old Eli is working on it right now."

"No, he was off to visit Widow Lapp, then pick up some supplies."

"Hmm… Think about it, though. You know as many people in the district as Old Eli. You've installed solar panels on nearly all the Amish homes. Surely you know someone who could rent a room to her. As for a job, there's always somebody in our community looking for help."

Elijah stood, dumped his coffee into the small sink and rinsed out the cup. His *bruder* was completely misreading his intentions, but perhaps he was right about one thing.

Perhaps he could do something to help Faith and Hannah.

"Let me know how the courting goes," Thomas called out as Elijah walked back through the barn.

He didn't bother responding.

Thomas would tease until he found something else to distract him. It was his way. By the time it reached their *mamm*, the story would have morphed into something completely crazy…something like Elijah had asked Faith to marry him.

Ha!

He knew when a woman didn't enjoy his company.

It had been plain as the snow falling around them that he irritated her in every way. Even when he wasn't talking she seemed put out with him. It was almost as if his very breathing had grated on her nerves.

She thought he was a know-it-all. What had she called him? A busybody. He couldn't help it if he had better ideas than she did. He was a businessman. It was his job to solve problems.

That was it. He was a problem solver.

Faith's problem was she needed a safe place to live and a way to support her daughter.

They were Amish. Supporting Hannah wouldn't be a problem. Everyone would pitch in. They might not be well-off, but neither would they lack for the basic necessities. Faith had struck him as a proud person, though—not proud in the sense of crowing about one's accomplishments, but too proud to do nothing while others helped.

Elijah understood that a person needed to feel like they were pulling their own weight. Didn't he have two *schweschdern* who still worked, even after having children? True, it was in their home, but still, it was satisfying to them.

Deborah had said at Christmas that quilting helped her to keep her sanity, what with the constant work of six children. "You can see the progress of a quilt. It has a beginning and an end to it. You feel like you've accomplished something when you cut the last thread, unlike doing the dinner dishes, which are dirty again the next morning."

His *mamm* had admonished Deborah that raising children was certainly accomplishing something— something far more important than sewing a quilt—

but Elijah had understood what his *schweschder* was getting at.

Lily, his oldest *schweschder*, had piped up with an old proverb he remembered his *mammi* saying.

How did it go?

Keeping a neat house is like threading beads on a string with no knot in it.

He sympathized with what his *schweschdern* had tried to say, and he suspected that Faith felt the same.

He didn't know her exact situation. She was quite young to be a widow, and to raise a child on one's own was no easy thing. What had happened to her parents? Didn't she have siblings? And what had she meant when she'd said it hadn't been safe living with her husband's parents?

He couldn't begin to imagine what kind of home her in-laws had provided that would be dangerous to a woman and child. It made him angry to think of such a thing, so instead he turned his thoughts away, headed to his barn and hitched up Boots.

There was someone he needed to visit, and he needed to do so before the buses to Michigan started running again.

Chapter Three

Faith couldn't believe when a few hours later Elijah returned. She just couldn't believe it. She'd actually felt guilty after he'd left, worried that she'd been rude and abrupt. Now he was back, and she was thinking that perhaps she hadn't been rude enough.

Unfortunately he arrived as Mary Ann was serving dinner to her family. Of course, Mary Ann insisted on setting another plate at the table. The bishop had eight children ranging from seven to nineteen, so dinnertime was a boisterous affair. Moreover, two of the girls had taken a real liking to Hannah, who returned their attentions with exuberant smiles and the occasional chuckle.

She would have enjoyed the meal if it hadn't been for Elijah hovering nearby. What was with him? Why did he care about what happened to her? Throughout the meal, Faith would look up to catch him studying her.

By the time they'd finished eating the chicken and dumplings, fresh bread and carrots, she felt she was sitting on eggshells. Plainly he'd come to say something to her. She wished he'd just get on with it.

"Why don't we head to the sitting room while the

children clean up the dishes." Mary Ann's eyes practically twinkled. The woman apparently hadn't picked up on Faith's discomfort.

And really, why was she uncomfortable around Elijah? He had done nothing but help her, and though he voiced his opinions a bit too bluntly, she was grateful to him for giving her a ride the night before.

The bishop's two oldest girls whisked Hannah away for a bath. Faith's arms felt empty, but she was also grateful for the break. There was no doubt that the girls knew what they were doing with a baby. As Mary Ann had explained, "They've had a lot of experience with the younger ones."

Once the four adults were settled in the sitting room, Old Eli pulled out an unlit pipe, clamped it between his teeth and motioned for Elijah to share his big news. That's what he'd called it—big news. Then he'd smelled the chicken and dumplings and the urgency of the thing had gone out of it. Just like that. Poof. Now his stomach was full, and he was obviously quite eager to share his news.

"I was discussing Faith's situation with Thomas…"

"What?" Faith's voice rose an octave. She pulled it down with some effort. "You discussed my situation with…who?"

"Thomas is Elijah's older *bruder*," Mary Ann explained. "He's a *gut* man. I hope you have the chance to meet him. Six children and a sweet wife. Go ahead, Elijah… You were saying."

Faith attempted to skewer him with a glare, but he failed to notice.

"Thomas suggested that perhaps there was a way

for you to stay in Shipshe, that maybe you could find what you were looking for here."

"I found what I'm looking for in Mio."

"*Ya*, right. The land to the north, the land of the frozen tundra…"

Faith felt her face turning red, Elijah sputtered to a stop and Mary Ann cleared her throat.

"You were saying…" Old Eli encouraged him onward with a motion of his pipe.

"Thomas suggested that I ask around. He said I know nearly as many people as you do."

"*Ya*, it's true."

"At first I thought of Daniel and Tabitha Miller…"

Mary Beth shook her head. "I'm sure Tabitha would be happy to help, but she has her mother to look after."

"And Daniel's had some trouble with his boys, who are suspender deep in their *rumspringa* at the moment." Old Eli shrugged. "I've no doubt it will work its way out in the end, but in the meantime the road could be a little bumpy."

"Right, so I was driving away from there after realizing it wasn't the ideal situation, and that's when I thought of Leslie Stolzfus."

Faith wanted to melt into the couch. She wanted to find Hannah, run to the room she was borrowing and shut the door. Had Elijah told her situation to every family in the local community? She didn't consider herself a proud person, but she did value her privacy. What was he thinking?

"Ah," Mary Ann said.

"Hmm…" Old Eli stared down at his pipe, even as he set his rocker to rocking.

A quiet descended on the room, pulling Faith out of

her embarrassment. Mary Ann had closed her eyes, as if in prayer. Old Eli continued to study his pipe. Which left her no one to look at except Elijah, who winked conspiratorially.

Mary Ann and Old Eli tossed the idea back and forth.

"It could work," Mary Ann said.

"I probably should have thought of it myself."

"She has two extra rooms."

"And a kind spirit."

"She's even talked about renting out to *Englischers* wanting to experience the Plain lifestyle."

"This would be better than that."

"This would be perfect."

Both Mary Ann and Old Eli looked to Faith, who had no idea what to say.

Old Eli stopped rocking, leaned forward and propped his elbows on his knees. "Elijah has a good grasp of the members of our community. There are many who would be willing to help, like the Kings, but few have an ideal situation for a young mother and child. Leslie, though…"

He looked to Mary Ann, who nodded, then reached over and covered Faith's hand with her own. "Leslie is a kindred spirit. If you'd like to stay, I think you should talk to her."

"Stay?"

"I suppose that's the real question here." Old Eli's demeanor became quite somber. His expression turned thoughtful, and he waited until silence had settled upon the room. Finally, he nodded toward her and asked, "What do you want, Faith?"

"What do I want?"

"If you'd rather travel on to Mio, the buses should begin running again tomorrow. I checked with the ticket salesman while I was in town today, and he assured me that buses would be leaving from the Mercantile in the early afternoon. However, he didn't believe you'd be able to reach Mio right away. He thought you'd probably get as far as Lansing. Apparently everything north of there is still closed."

"But I need to get to Mio."

"Right."

Everyone waited and watched her.

Faith didn't know what to think, and she certainly didn't know what to say. She felt like Alice who had fallen down the rabbit hole.

It was Mary Ann who rescued her, who offered her at least a glimmer of light through the fog of confusion.

"You think and pray about it, dear. Pray about staying here in Shipshe and whether it's the best thing for you and Hannah. In the meantime, it wouldn't hurt to go tomorrow morning and speak with Leslie. The bus doesn't depart until after lunch, which gives you plenty of time to make a decision."

Plenty of time to make a decision.

The clock on the wall ticked toward 7:00 p.m.

She had sixteen hours to decide where she wanted to raise her daughter.

Faith glanced up and saw only kindness and compassion in Mary Ann's eyes. Old Eli was looking at her as her father once had, and the memory brought a lump to her throat. But it was the expression on Elijah's face that gave her pause. If she wasn't mistaken, he was eagerly awaiting her answer.

Why? Why did he care?

Finally she said, "Sure. *Ya.* I suppose I could talk to her. It can't hurt, I guess."

The smile that erupted on Elijah's face reached all the way to his eyes, which she again noticed were a blue as deep as a summer sky. She supposed many women would be flattered to have Elijah's attention.

Not her.

She didn't need another man.

And she didn't need to be rescued.

But she did need a place to live, and it didn't look like she'd get to Mio anytime soon. Was *Gotte* closing that door? Where did that expression even come from? She wasn't sure it was in the Bible.

But she did believe that *Gotte* guided her path. So it was settled. In the morning, she would go to see Leslie.

Mary Ann stood and straightened her apron. "I best see to the *kinner.* I'll check on Hannah, too. Eli, both of the boys were wanting help from you with a school project. They're waiting at the table. Faith, would you mind seeing Elijah out?"

Which pretty much meant walking him across the room. Faith was quite sure he could find the way himself. She didn't want to appear rude, though, so she nodded, stood and walked Elijah to the front door. He snagged his hat, scarf and gloves from the peg on the wall where he'd left them.

She found herself looking up into those startling blue eyes. She wasn't used to looking up at anyone. Even her husband had been an inch shorter.

"I can take you to Leslie's in the morning."

"That won't be necessary. I'm sure Old Eli…"

"He meets with the church leaders on Friday mornings, though he'll cancel if you ask him to."

"*Nein.* I wouldn't want that."

"It's settled, then. I'll pick you up at nine." He leaned slightly toward her and lowered his voice, though they were the only ones in the room. "I'm not trying to be in your business. It's just that… It seems like providence that I was driving by when you needed someone."

"Providence?"

"*Ya.* As if *Gotte* intended for us to meet."

"Oh. I don't know…"

"I'm not reading too much into it." He smiled now, and she realized that if he wasn't bossing her around she might actually like him. "It's not as if I think it was a sign that we should begin courting."

"Courting?" Heat flooded Faith's cheeks. "I've known you all of twenty-four hours, Elijah King. Not to mention, my priority for the foreseeable future is Hannah."

"*Ya.* That's what I was saying. I'm not reading too much into it."

He reached out and lightly squeezed her arm. Faith nearly jumped out of her skin. If Elijah noticed, he didn't say anything, which was good because she was mortally embarrassed about the entire turn of this conversation.

He stepped out into the cold, snowy evening, and she firmly shut the door behind him. Faith stood there and watched out the window as he walked over to the barn. What was the name of his buggy horse? Boots. A few minutes later he guided Boots out of the barn, shut the door and climbed up into the buggy. Faith stood there watching after him, long after he'd disappeared into the night.

In that moment, she could almost envision what her

life might have been like—if her parents were still alive, if she hadn't married so quickly, if Jonas hadn't died. She might have had a normal life, with a husband and a horse named Boots.

But she had no husband or horse or home.

She couldn't go back and change the past, but perhaps tomorrow, she could settle on a place to live.

The next day dawned with bright sunshine splashing over the snowy landscape. Elijah caught himself whistling as he cleaned out his buggy, swapped out the old blanket for a cleaner one he'd borrowed from his sister-in-law and picked up loose trash that had accumulated on the floor of the buggy. By the time he reached Old Eli's place, fifteen minutes early, the buggy was toasty warm.

Faith must have been watching for him because as soon as he drove up, she stuck her head out the door and motioned for him to wait. Less than a minute later, she hurried out to the buggy.

"Let me help you up."

"I've got it."

"At least let me hold Hannah."

She passed the bundled child to him. Apparently Mary Beth had been sharing her baby things as Hannah was wearing a slightly used coat, had a newly knitted cap covering her head and was wrapped in a fleece blanket. She smiled at him and bounced in his arms.

And that was the moment Elijah first wondered if he was in trouble.

Looking into Hannah's eyes, which were a perfect replica of her mother's, then looking up at Faith, Elijah realized he might be sinking into something he didn't understand. Was it even possible that he was falling for Faith Yoder? He'd known her less than two days. He must be feeling *narrisch* because only someone who wasn't thinking straight would have romantic notions about a complete stranger—and one who had no intention of courting on top of that.

Ack.

He had absolutely no common sense when it came to women.

But then again, the heart yearned for what the heart yearned for. He realized in that moment that it wasn't a head thing. It was a heart-and-soul thing.

He passed Hannah back to Faith, murmured to Boots, "Behave yourself, please," and hurried to the other side of the buggy.

"Thank you for taking us to see Leslie."

"No problem."

"I'm sure you have work to do… Didn't you say you owned a big business?"

"I probably didn't use the word *big*, but it is normally quite busy. All my jobs halted for the weather, though. Can't have people working in treacherous conditions. I suspect we'll be back up to speed by tomorrow."

Faith glanced out the window at the bright sunshine, then looked back at him.

"*Ya*, I know it's sunny now, but we have to give the snow time to melt off the roof. Wouldn't want anyone sliding down into a snowbank."

He proceeded to tell her how he'd become interested in solar panels, starting out as a one-man business and growing past that quickly, all due to the way their community had embraced solar energy.

Faith seemed interested in everything he had to say.

Finally he asked, "Did your community—your old community—use solar power?"

"*Nein.* But even if they had, I don't think my father-in-law would have allowed it. He's not much one for change."

Her voice had taken on a plaintive tone, and he quickly changed the subject. He was interested in hearing of her past, but he didn't want to put a damper on the morning. So he pointed out the homes of people in their community as they drove toward Leslie's. He tried to think of a funny anecdote to go with each farm they passed, which wasn't so hard. They had a lot of characters in their church district.

When he turned into the lane leading to a small new house set back from the road, he heard her pull in a sharp breath.

"Too small?"

"I wasn't expecting...something so nice."

"*Ya.* Leslie built this place with her husband. They were downsizing from a bigger farm, entering their golden years as she puts it. I installed her solar panels. Six months after they moved in, her husband, John, was diagnosed with cancer. He died only three months later."

"What are the building pads for?"

"They'd planned to open the property up as a bed-and-breakfast—perhaps build cabins around this circular drive. Now she's not sure if she can do it on her own. She doesn't even know if she should continue living here by herself. Leslie's not really old enough for a *Daddi* house, though her children have offered. I think she's lonely and a little at loose ends."

Faith remained quiet through his entire explanation. He wondered what she was thinking. That this wouldn't be a *gut* place to live? Or that it would?

He called out, "Whoa, Boots," set the brake, then hopped down to loop the reins around a long hitching rail in front of Leslie's porch. By the time he made it around to Faith's side of the buggy, she'd already scrambled out and was standing there, holding baby Hannah tightly against her chest and looking at the house.

He tried to see it as she did.

The outside sported a light gray paint with white trim.

The porch extended across the front and down the east side—big enough for rocking chairs and plants and a small table that Leslie liked to place a pitcher of lemonade on during the summer.

The place was spick-and-span, without even a hint of mud on the porch. "She keeps a clean house," he explained as he cupped her elbow and guided her up the porch steps. Before they could knock on the door, Leslie had opened it up and motioned them inside.

"The sunshine is nice, but it's still quite brisk out there. You must be Faith, and this is…"

"Hannah." Faith moved the baby into her other arm.

"Let's go to the kitchen. It's cozy warm and has the best light in the morning."

Elijah thought the kitchen looked like something out of a storybook. The walls were painted a soft yellow, a table for six sat in an alcove surrounded on three sides by windows and the smell of freshly brewed coffee filled the room.

Leslie reminded Elijah of the quintessential Amish

mammi—gray hair peeking out from her *kapp*, fresh white apron, short and round with smile wrinkles fanning out from her eyes. He knew, though, that she wasn't the typical grandma. Leslie had always enjoyed trying new things. She was one of the first to sign up for solar panels, and six weeks after John's death, she'd started putting out inquiries about hosting *Englisch* families. Then her plans for the bed-and-breakfast had stalled, her enthusiasm had waned and she'd been unable to move forward.

Perhaps it was grief.

He understood that she missed John terribly. She'd even told Elijah once that she wasn't sure what the purpose of her days were. Why was she still here, but John was gone? Why was his life complete, when hers was supposed to keep going? None of it made sense to her, and so she had decided to pause and wait for answers from *Gotte*.

Once she'd served everyone coffee and taken Hannah onto her lap, she got down to business. "Elijah tells me you're looking for a place to live. I won't push my nose into your business, but I feel that I do need to know something of your background."

"I understand." Faith glanced uncertainly at Elijah.

"Would you like me to leave? If you'd rather this be a private conversation—"

"Of course not. I was trying to think of where to begin."

"At the beginning is usually best, dearie." Leslie raised Hannah to her shoulder, having already slipped a clean diaper over her dress as a burp cloth. How did women do that? Did they pull clean diapers out of thin air?

Then Faith began talking, and Elijah forgot all about Leslie's grandmothering abilities.

Faith was an only child.

Her parents had perished in a buggy accident.

She'd met Jonas the next year. He suffered from some medical condition she didn't know about, and by the time they were aware of it, he'd passed. She'd been three months pregnant at the time.

Elijah thought there was more to that part of the story. Faith had paused, stared down into her coffee, then drained the cup and skipped to the end.

"I didn't realize when I married Jonas what his family was like. Jonas was a kind man, but his *dat*—he had a problem with alcohol."

Leslie tsked and rubbed Hannah's back in slow, smooth circles.

"The bishop tried several times to convince Gerald to go into counseling, but he adamantly refused to admit he had a problem. As for Jonas's *mamm*, well, Sara learned to stay out of his way."

"Not so easy for a young widow with a child."

"Exactly. I seemed to…" Faith pressed her lips together, glanced at Elijah and continued. "I seemed to remind him of the death of his son. He… I think he blamed me."

"Why would he do such a thing?" Elijah had remained quiet up to that point, but the cruelness of what she was describing bothered him. He never could understand how some people lacked compassion.

"I don't think… He wasn't in his right mind. His drinking worsened after Jonas's death."

"And your bishop? Surely he was sympathetic to your situation."

"He offered to find another place within the district for us to stay, until the living conditions with Gerald and Sara improved. The thing was that I don't believe it ever was going to improve. I think they had been living that way a long time. It explained why Jonas's *bruders* had moved so far away."

"I am indeed sorry for the trouble you've endured, Faith." Leslie reached across and patted her hand. "We can't understand *Gotte*'s ways. The prophet Isaiah said that *His ways are not our ways*. I do believe *Gotte* has the ability to bless us in spite of our trials. I'm learning that truth myself, though not every day feels that way."

Faith didn't argue, though she didn't look quite convinced either.

"In the end, I decided moving would be better, and Gerald—he was happy to see us go. I think Sara was relieved. She loves Hannah, but she was worried about my raising a child in that home. She said as much to me once."

"So you began watching the *Budget*…looking for a home and job." Elijah wondered what kind of strength that must take. Sure, he'd purchased his own farm and started his own business, but he'd always had the support of family. Faith had been completely alone, and she'd still found the courage to make her own way.

"I answered the ad for Mio, Michigan. Of course, I realized how far north it was, but I didn't think we'd be snowed out before we even reached there. And now… Honestly, now I'm not sure what to do. Mary Ann and Old Eli have been so kind, and their *doschdern* have taken a real liking to Hannah."

"They're *gut* people," Leslie agreed. She moved the

now-sleeping Hannah to the crook of her arm. "Tell me what kind of work you plan to do."

Elijah sat back, at ease for perhaps the first time since he'd seen Faith standing in the swirl of snow outside the Mercantile. Things seemed to be going well between her and Leslie, and he could picture her living in their community, doing a little side business of baking or quilting or sewing. All that was left was to work out the details.

He would give her time to settle into her new life. Then if this spark he thought existed between them persisted, he could ask her out. His dreams of a wife and family popped back into his head. Was it possible that his future was back on track?

Perhaps his New Year's resolution hadn't been so crazy after all.

Everything was turning out exactly as he dreamed it would.

Except now that he thought about it, Faith was looking at him quite oddly. She acted as if she was about to share some startling news. Her shoulders had tensed, and she was clutching her mug as if someone might wrestle it from her hands.

What was she not telling them?

When she began to speak, Elijah had the ridiculous urge to clap his hands over his ears. In the space of a heartbeat, the dream of his perfect little Amish family popped like a child's balloon.

Chapter Four

Faith's mouth felt suddenly dry. Elijah was sitting back and watching her as if this was a done deal, as if all that was left to figure out was when she would move in. But Faith knew that moving in with someone was a big step—it was a major decision for both her and Leslie. And the fact that her work wasn't exactly traditional might be the thing that put a stick in the spokes of the buggy wheel.

"When I took the job in Mio, I agreed to do farm work and the like." She pulled in a deep breath as she wiped her palms against her dress. "That's not what I do, though. That's not what I'm *gut* at."

Leslie looked interested.

Elijah looked mildly concerned.

"I draw up business plans." When no one spoke, she added, "For Amish companies, mostly, but also Mennonite and *Englisch*."

"I don't understand." Elijah set his coffee cup aside and rested his elbows on the table.

"And I didn't know there was such a thing." Leslie

cocked her head to the side. "Do you mean you take care of the accounting books?"

"I can do that, yes. But it's not the bulk of what I do—or did, before I met Jonas. Where we lived in Sugarcreek, my *dat* was *gut* with business ledgers and such, so I grew up around numbers and understood accounting terms well before I finished school. By the time I'd worked with him a few years, I could run a profit/loss statement, five-year projection, help identify and set attainable goals, do a market analysis…"

Elijah held up a hand to stop her. "Amish businesses asked for that?"

"*Ya.* Many did."

"None of the businessmen…"

Leslie cleared her throat and tossed him a pointed look.

Elijah tried again. "None of the business men or *women* I know would even understand what those things are."

"Which is exactly why it's a unique and needed service to local businesses."

"But if they don't know what it is, why would they pay for it?"

"In the beginning, I suppose because they trusted my *dat* and were already using his services. It was natural for them to trust me. Once we were successful with a handful of businesses, word spread."

Leslie glanced down at Hannah, then back up at Faith. "Why did you ever leave Sugarcreek? Why leave Ohio at all if you had such a *gut* business built up?"

"Because I fell in love?" Faith felt her right eye twitch, something she absolutely hated, but it happened whenever she was nervous. She fought the urge to close her eyes and press her fingertips against the twitching muscle. "Maybe because I was naive, or maybe... I guess maybe the pain of being in Sugarcreek became too much. After my parents' deaths, everywhere I turned reminded me of them, of their passing. I met Jonas, he asked me to wed and we moved to the Fort Wayne area—Adams County, to be exact."

Elijah was now frowning in an almost comical way. Obviously he didn't approve of her or her work plans. He sat back, crossed his arms and refused to meet her eyes. "Can't say as you'll be able to make a living doing that here in Shipshe."

"And how do you know that, Elijah King?" Leslie ducked her chin, gave him an impatient look and tsked all at once.

"I have a successful business, don't I? Yet, I've never had a business plan. Sounds like a bunch of hoopla to me."

"Hoopla?" Faith's nervousness gave way to irritation.

"Market analysis? Who needs market analysis? You look around, see a need and meet the need. That's all the business plan a person has to have—that and a *gut* work ethic will result in success."

"I don't know about that." Leslie stood, placed Hannah in Faith's arms, then refilled their coffee cups. "I've been rather stuck in my own business plans. It's possible that I could use exactly what you're describing."

Faith's spirits lifted. She'd never dared to mention her business abilities to Jonas's parents, and in truth, she'd missed doing the work. Gerald had made it quite clear that a woman's sole purpose was to care for the home and children. He'd described the women in their community who owned businesses as "putting on airs" and had suggested that their husbands needed to be more firm with them.

But she'd missed it. She could see that now. Helping people be successful in the things they wanted to do was fulfilling. The fact that she was usually paid well for it was an added bonus.

Leslie tapped her fingernails against the side of her mug. "Then again, Elijah has a point that folks in Shipshe have never heard of such a thing. You might have to start over, from the ground up."

"What do you mean?"

"Start with the accounting, something that many businesses admit they need help with. Amish men and *women*…" She emphasized the last word, throwing a glance at Elijah and then refocusing on Faith. "Amish men and women aren't usually *gut* with the practical sides of business. That's a stereotype for sure and certain, and yet I've seen it many times myself. I've seen it in myself."

She paused, looking out her kitchen window. "Why do you think I have building pads with no buildings? I like the idea of hosting *Englischers*, but I don't know how to proceed, or even if I should. I could invest what little funds I have, only to have my B and B flop."

"But it doesn't have to be that uncertain…" Faith sat up straighter, feeling an old familiar buzz shoot through her veins. "We can analyze how other similar businesses have done in neighboring communities."

"I don't know that there are any."

"Which is easy enough to find on the internet."

"I don't have a computer."

"But the library does. It's where I've always done

my research. A market analysis could be just the thing to either give you the confidence you need to continue with what you've started or send you in a different direction."

Elijah threw up his hands. "Libraries and research and market analysis. Whew. All too fancy for me. I'm just a small business owner."

Faith crossed her arms though she knew it made her look defensive. She was feeling defensive, so looking that way was fine with her. In truth, she was stung by Elijah's sarcastic tone. She glanced at Leslie, who was looking at Elijah as if he were wearing his hat upside down. At least she wasn't alone in her irritation.

Elijah shook his head, then stood and pushed his chair in, raising his hands in a gesture of surrender. "I best go and check on Boots," he said and stomped from the room.

Faith watched him go, uncertain what bothered her more—his abrupt change in mood or the fact that everything about her seemed to irritate him. Why should she care? She shouldn't. She barely knew Elijah King, and she certainly didn't need his approval.

Finally she turned to Leslie. "Seems I managed to put a twist in his suspenders."

"Oh, honey, it's not about you. Men like Elijah, they mean well, but they have trouble seeing women in different roles. No doubt he was picturing you with a quilting loom in front of you."

"I'm not a very *gut* quilter."

"Well, I could teach you, but if it's not the thing you love to do, then lessons won't help much. Now, tell me more about what would convince you to stay in Shipshewana, because I think you'd be a fine addition to our community."

Thirty minutes later they'd hammered out the details of Faith and Hannah coming to live with Leslie. They decided to try it on a temporary basis, and if either weren't completely happy with the arrangement there would be no harm done.

"I'm quite sure the job in Mio will still be there," Faith admitted. "And the woman told me she wouldn't be offended if I changed my mind. She failed to mention that I might have trouble even getting there."

"I don't know what *Gotte* has in store for you, dear, but I'm happy to be your landing spot until you figure that out."

"But what about rent? I won't be able to pay you right away."

"You'll pay me when you can. That will work just fine."

Leslie went to the barn to let Elijah know Faith was ready, while Faith stayed in the house changing Hannah's nappie. For the first time in a long time, the heavy cloud of despair that had pressed down on her since Jonas's death seemed to have lifted.

She picked Hannah up, held her high in the air, then brought her close so their noses were touching. Hannah laughed, then fisted both of her hands against Faith's face.

"Perhaps this is where we're supposed to be, baby girl." She glanced around the house—freshly painted walls, sunshine streaming through the windows, the sound of a bird chirping outside. It was almost too *gut* to be true. A peaceful, safe place for them to live.

True, Leslie was virtually a stranger to her.

But so was the woman in Mio.

For the moment, she needed the kindness of strangers, and she was grateful that she'd found that in Shipshe. She would be a fool to pass it up. Wouldn't she?

She pulled herself from her musings and hurried outside.

Elijah held Hannah as she climbed into the buggy.

"See you in the morning," Leslie said, leaning in and patting Hannah. "And don't worry about cribs and bedding and such. We'll make do."

Elijah was unusually quiet as they made their way back to Old Eli's. Faith could sense his irritation, but she couldn't bring herself to address what had caused it. Obviously he disapproved of her. What more was there to say? Except she did need to say one thing, even if it hurt her pride to do so.

Clearing her throat, she cornered herself in the buggy and studied him. "I want to thank you."

"What for?"

"Taking me to see Leslie, thinking of her in the first place, slowing down and offering me a ride during the snowstorm."

She might have imagined it, but it seemed that Elijah's expression softened at the mention of their first meeting. Had it really been only two days ago? She already felt as if she'd known him for ages.

He squared his shoulders, focused on the road, but finally gave in to the urge to set her straight. And she knew from the first sentence that was what he intended to do.

"I'm happy that things are going to work out with Leslie, and that you and Hannah are staying..."

"But..."

"But why can't you try your hand at something more traditional?"

"More traditional?"

"For your work. You won't need much money, not really. The community will help."

"And what if I want to pay my own way?"

"Then why can't you do it baking or, or…"

"Quilting?" She almost laughed. Leslie had been right. Elijah, for all his new ideas and solar panels, was unable to picture a woman in a less-than-traditional occupation. "Don't you think Shipshe has enough Amish quilters?"

"I don't know about that. My *schweschder* Deborah seems to do well with it. Not sure you can have too many Amish quilters or quilts, though maybe you could go to the library and research the exact numbers."

"Now you're mocking me."

Elijah picked his hat up, then squashed it back on his head, but he didn't deny what she'd said.

"It's just that I'd think you would want something more certain for Hannah."

"Don't do that."

"Don't do what?"

"Pretend you know what's best for my *doschder*." Faith was relieved to see them pull into Old Eli's place. She couldn't get out of the buggy fast enough. In fact, she wanted to tell him to drop her off at the mailbox, but she knew he wouldn't do any such thing. So instead she focused on pulling the blanket more tightly around Hannah, who immediately began to fuss.

"Can't see as I was doing that." Elijah raised his voice to be heard over Hannah's cries.

"Then perhaps you need glasses." Faith's temper

had complete control of her tongue now, and she knew that was dangerous. She closed her eyes, pictured Leslie's calm home and reined in her emotions. When Elijah stopped, instead of hopping out of the buggy, she waited for him to look at her.

"*Danki*, Elijah, for all you have done for us. I meant it when I said that earlier. But you're not responsible for my life or for Hannah's. We don't need your help, and I'd appreciate your respecting my wishes on this."

"What are you saying?"

"I'm saying that you should mind your own business. You know nothing about me, nothing about what is best for me or Hannah, and the last thing I need at this point in my life is a man telling me what I should do. That has not worked well for me in the past."

She waited for him to nod that he understood before hopping out of the buggy, and she couldn't have explained why tears stung her eyes as she hurried up the porch steps. Somehow she'd envisioned a friendship between them, but that wasn't going to happen. She needed friends who believed in her, who would support her decisions.

If she was going to stay in Shipshewana, and it seemed she was, then she'd do well to put distance between herself and Elijah King.

Elijah managed to stay away from Old Eli's the next day.

Sunday was an off-Sunday, so instead of going to church he headed over to his parents' place. With his two *bruders*, three *schweschdern* and their families, it was always a boisterous affair. After they'd eaten, the conversation turned to Faith and Hannah. Fortunately, he needed to check on the horses so he excused himself from the table.

Faith had told him to mind his own business, and he planned to do just that.

But their community was small and close-knit. He couldn't avoid news of Faith for long, and truthfully he was curious. She might not be the *fraa* whom he'd dreamed of, the woman that *Gotte* intended for him, but she was a neighbor whom he cared about.

He was embarrassed that he'd ever dreamed they could mean more to one another than that.

Woman in a snow globe indeed.

Perhaps he'd hit his head and knocked a few screws loose. Love didn't work that way. It didn't appear out of thin air—or even out of a snowy evening. Love was something that took time to cultivate. Even he, with his limited experience courting, knew that.

It was Monday morning when he heard from one of his employees, Jesse, that Faith had moved in with Leslie. Jesse's *fraa* had donated a cradle. "We won't be needing it since Beth can't have any more children." Jesse's wife had needed a special surgery after their last *kinder*, their eighth, was born.

The two men were carrying solar panels from Elijah's supply shed to his flatbed trailer. He'd had it built specifically to be pulled by his buggy. He'd even had it registered with the department of motor vehicles. And he hadn't needed a single business plan to know how to do those things. After he'd received his first ticket from a Shipshewana police officer for pulling an unregistered trailer, he'd taken care of everything.

Why couldn't Faith see that her idea was ludicrous? Amish businesses didn't need a business plan.

"Did you even hear what I just said?"

"Course I did."

"So you'll be there?"

"Be where?"

Jesse laughed. "Your mind is somewhere else today, my friend. I said that we're having a work day at Leslie's on Saturday, to build on a room for Faith and her *boppli*."

Elijah stopped halfway between the shed and the flatbed, holding three solar panels. "So she's staying… long-term, I mean. She must be if they're building on a room."

"Leslie said she was wanting to do it anyway, and it'll give Faith a little privacy. Rather like a *dawdi haus*, but attached."

"Huh." Elijah continued on to the trailer, carefully placed the panels on the stack already there, then proceeded to tie them down with straps and bungee cords. It made no difference to him whether Faith stayed for a week or twenty years.

He was happy for her, of course.

Everyone should have a home, a place where they felt safe.

His mind flashed back on what she'd said about her in-laws. There was something she hadn't shared. He was sure of it. Whatever it was, he was glad she was clear of the couple if they'd been that unkind.

An image flashed across his mind of Hannah reaching for his hat. She was a happy baby, and he was glad that she was in a cozy, safe home. Leslie would provide that, for sure and certain.

He made a mental note to clear his schedule the following Saturday. The least he could do was show up to help Leslie. He'd just find a way to stay out of Faith's path. Clearly what he'd thought was growing between them wasn't. It was all because of that New Year's resolution he'd made—as if one could decide to find a *fraa*, as if he had any say in such a thing happening.

He didn't.

And he probably wouldn't.

And the sooner he accepted that, the better.

The rest of the week seemed to drag by, though he was working on two new houses and one business. He found himself putting panels on upside down and forgetting to bill one client, and on Friday morning he even drove to the wrong job site.

He was distracted.

Who wouldn't be on a wintry week in January? Spring was still so far off, and everything was harder to do in the cold. He was grateful that he had only the one buggy horse to care for. The weather was cloudy but no additional snow fell. Elijah knew he should be grateful for that. Instead his restlessness increased, and he found himself putting in extra hours on the jobs. But working more didn't calm his agitated spirit.

"You're in a funk," his *bruder* declared one evening.

"*Ya*. What would you know about that?"

"Everyone gets in a funk at one time or another. The key is to figure out what's causing it, then do the opposite."

"Uh-huh. Maybe winter's causing it. How do I do the opposite?"

"You could take a trip to Sarasota."

Elijah snorted. "And hang out with a bunch of old folks? No thanks."

"You could volunteer for an MDS mission. They're

still sending crews to work on houses in Florida and Texas."

"Thomas, I work on houses all day, nearly every day. I can't imagine volunteering to ride in a van for twenty hours, so I could work on more houses."

"You are in a funk."

They were in Elijah's barn, working on a new dining room table for their *mamm*'s birthday. Aaron, Elijah's younger *bruder*, was working on a preacher's bench and chairs to go with the table. It was all supposed to be a big surprise, but something told Elijah that his *mamm* already knew what they were doing.

Thomas snapped his fingers. "I've got it. You need to start courting."

Elijah stared down at the file he was using to smooth out the side of the table. He briefly thought about chucking it at his *bruder*, but then he'd have to go and pick it up off the floor. So instead, he sighed and continued filing the wood.

"I heard a group of *youngies* have scheduled a driver. They're going up to Timber Ridge to ski on Friday."

When Elijah didn't rise to the bait, Thomas added, "You used to love to ski."

"I haven't skied in ten years."

"That long?"

"Yup. That long."

In truth the thought of riding in a van with a dozen eighteen-year-olds was enough to set his teeth on edge. Fortunately, Thomas took the hint and dropped the subject. Within a few minutes, they'd turned to safer topics—spring crops, the cost of seed and projected weather forecasts.

Elijah tossed and turned most of Friday night.

Finally he threw back the covers, padded to the kitchen and made himself a cup of coffee. One of the perks of being a bachelor in his own home was that he could keep whatever hours he liked.

"Not exactly a perk," he muttered to himself.

The home he had built was beautiful.

His business was successful

But he was unhappy on a fundamental level.

What was it Old Eli had preached on during their last service? Something about eating and drinking and birds.

He sipped his coffee, then stood and fetched his Bible from the table next to the couch. He read it rather infrequently, except for during Sunday service. He had good intentions of studying whatever passage Old Eli preached on, but then he got home, tossed the Bible onto the table and generally forgot about it until the next church meeting.

Not today, though.

Glancing out the window, where dawn was still a long way off, he suddenly needed to see the verses Old Eli had focused on. He stumbled his way through the Psalms, decided it wasn't there, then flipped back and forth in the New Testament before he finally found the passage in the book of Matthew, chapter six.

Take no thought for your life, what ye shall eat or what ye shall drink.

He didn't overly focus on such things. He certainly didn't stop to think about what there was to eat in his pantry. But perhaps that wasn't what the gospel writer had meant. If he were honest with himself, and what was the point in lying to yourself, his thoughts usually centered on his business, what was next on the work schedule and whether he'd done a good job on the last site.

Is not the life more than meat, and the body more than raiment?

Easy enough to say when you had plenty of meat and raiment. What was raiment, anyway? He read the verses again, decided the word meant *clothes*, and immediately thought of baby Hannah swaddled in her patched blanket.

Behold the fowls of the air...your heavenly Father feedeth them. Are ye not much better than they?

The words followed him through the chores that he finished as the sun was coming up, then as he hitched Boots to the buggy and finally as he drove toward Leslie's.

Round and round they went.

Are ye not much better than they?

Of course. He understood that *Gotte* loved and cared for them. It was just that he'd fallen into the habit of caring for himself. He'd always had an independent streak, and it had only grown as the years had passed.

He was confident that he could and would continue to work hard and provide for himself—at least as long as he was healthy.

He had built a fine home and farm, a *gut* business, a productive life. But what he couldn't do was provide himself a soul mate. Only *Gotte* could do that. And wasn't life more than what they ate or what they wore? Those things were meaningless if you had no one to share them with.

Faith had someone to share those things with—she had Hannah. True, it sounded as if she'd endured her share of hardship, but her confidence, even her happiness, came from that little baby girl. She wasn't living for herself. She was living for Hannah.

As he neared Leslie's place, slowing to fall into the line of buggies that was trundling down the lane for the work day, he realized that he'd misunderstood his feelings for Faith. He wasn't aggravated with her for having a different kind of business. He wasn't irritated with her for following a different plan for her life than he would have recommended.

Plain and simple, he was jealous.

And he'd allowed his jealousy to mar what might have grown into a treasured friendship.

Which meant he had one important thing to do today, and it didn't involve the work on Leslie's addition. He needed to set things straight with Faith.

He needed to apologize.

Chapter Five

Faith was a little embarrassed that Leslie was insisting on adding on a room to her house.

"We don't mind staying in your guest room."

"It's too small for you and Hannah."

"But what if…" Faith stopped, trying to think how to tactfully express her fears.

"If it doesn't work out?" Leslie smiled as she added more sandwiches to the platter they were making for workers.

The women would arrive in another hour, and they'd also bring food. Faith had been to many work days in her life, but she'd never been the recipient of one. It was all a bit overwhelming…and humbling.

"If it doesn't work, I could always rent out the room as part of my B and B plan. And if that doesn't work— yes, I realize it might not—then it will make my house easier to sell. It was a bit small for the average Amish family, that's for certain." Leslie turned toward her, placing a hand on each of Faith's shoulders. "But for now I'm doing it because I want you and Hannah to be comfortable."

Tears stung Faith's eyes, and she pretended that she needed to check on Hannah, who was sleeping soundly in their tiny room. Leslie was correct that the room was small. It had initially been designed to accommodate a visiting grandchild—not as a permanent space for a mother and baby. The twin bed, small dresser and cradle took up all the available space. But Faith didn't mind that. At the moment she could have collapsed on that bed and slept for three days. She didn't, of course. No one would sleep through a work day at their own house—unless they were ill, which she wasn't.

The morning passed in a blur of activity. The ring of hammers and saws, the occasional song as men worked in rhythm to a hymn and the laughter of children running across the yard filled the morning.

"*Gotte* has blessed us with *gut* weather."

She jumped at the sound of Elijah's voice.

"I didn't realize you were here."

"Of course I'm here." He took the platter of sandwiches from her. They walked outside and paused to look at the construction. It resembled a barn raising more than anything else, though, of course, it wasn't nearly that large.

They stood there in the bright January sunshine, shoulder to shoulder, studying the structure that was quickly appearing before their eyes—it was a work of love and grace, that was for certain.

"It's amazing what we can do when we work together, and *Gotte* has given us a fine day for it, *ya*? We've much to be grateful for."

Elijah's voice was close, and for reasons she couldn't understand, it caused a cascade of goose bumps to dance down her arms. She felt tears prick her eyes and murmured something about needing to get the platter of sandwiches to the barn.

Instead of picking up on the fact that she wanted to be alone, Elijah insisted on carrying the tray to the serving table in the barn.

Faith hurried back into the kitchen to retrieve the two cakes Leslie had baked. As she made her way across the yard to the barn, she realized that Elijah was right. The day was sunny, which helped to mitigate the slight north wind. The children barely noticed the cold, and the men were grateful for the sunshine. Most of the mothers and babes were in the barn setting up the luncheon.

All the people introduced themselves to Faith, but by the time the meal was over and men were returning to work, she couldn't have remembered a single name.

"Your *boppli* is about the same age as my Mary."

Faith turned around to see a woman close to her own age, holding a babe to her shoulder and rubbing her back in soft circles.

"I'm Deborah, Elijah's *schweschder*."

"Oh. It's *gut* to meet you."

"Elijah told me how you two met. Sounds like the beginning of a romance novel." Her eyes twinkled. "Your babe's name is Hannah, right?"

"*Ya*. She turned a year last month."

"Small for her age. Well, don't worry about that. She'll catch up. How does she sleep?"

"*Gut*."

"Then she's getting plenty to eat. As my *mamm* says, if a babe sleeps well, then whatever you're doing is working."

"I think I'd like your *mamm*."

"She couldn't be here today as she had a doctor's appointment."

"I hope everything's okay."

"Fine. It's a yearly checkup, and she didn't want to reschedule. She's looking forward to meeting you at church tomorrow after hearing so much about you."

When Faith raised her eyebrows in surprise, Deborah laughed. "Elijah rarely talks about a woman. You've sparked an interest in him that we haven't seen in quite a while."

"Mostly I aggravate him."

"About your job?" Deborah laughed again and switched her baby to her other shoulder. "Don't look so surprised that he told us. As I said, not many women interest him, but you've certainly done so."

"He doesn't approve. He told me so quite plainly. He asked why I didn't try baking or quilting… Say, are you the *schweschder* that quilts?"

"I am, but I also love doing it. Now, as for baking, I'm less than stellar at that. My cookies come out burnt on the edges and my cakes resemble pudding on the inside."

Faith relaxed for the first time that day. She recognized a kindred spirit in Elijah's *schweschder*. It felt *gut* to talk to another woman—another young mom.

"He was quite opinionated about what I should or shouldn't be doing to earn a living."

"If there's one thing Elijah has in abundance, it's confidence. He's used to being right, and often he is. But that doesn't mean he understands your situation."

She reached out, squeezed Faith's arm and leaned closer to whisper. "Don't give up on him. He's stubborn, but he's one of the *gut* ones."

And then one of Deborah's other children called out to her from the other side of the barn, so she hurried away.

But Faith heard those words as she cleared the dishes and peeked at the work being done on her new room.

Don't give up on him.

He's stubborn, but he's one of the gut *ones.*

And perhaps that's why when Elijah found her later that afternoon, her aggravation toward him had cooled somewhat. She was standing in the living room, watching the men pass back and forth in front of the window. Though she wanted to be out with them, she needed to stay inside in case Hannah woke up. Most of the women had gone home so they'd be there as schoolchildren returned. Already half of the buggies had cleared out. Leslie was in the barn speaking with the few remaining women.

"I was looking for you."

Faith startled at the sound of Elijah's voice. Pulling her shawl closer around her shoulders, she turned from the living room window and studied him. "I had to put Hannah down for a nap."

"Is she doing okay with all this…hoopla?"

"Oh *ya*. She fell asleep with one group hammering on the adjacent wall and another on the roof over her head."

"They're adding the drywall on the inside of the walls now."

"I can't believe they've done the entire thing in a day," Faith said.

"*Ya*, we're fast workers. Between you and me, most everyone here was happy to have a day away from the farm. You know how it gets in the winter. We all have a little spring fever."

"Long way until spring."

"Don't I know it." Elijah stuffed his hands in his pockets, took a step toward her and stopped. Blowing out a breath, he looked at her and smiled. "I need to apologize."

"*Nein*, you don't."

"I do. The day I brought you out here, I was rude. I was being a busybody." A soft chuckle escaped his lips. "You called me on it, and I deserved it."

"Actually I shouldn't have. You'd been very kind. I should have kept my opinion to myself."

"Why would you do that?"

He walked over next to where she stood, and for just a minute, she thought he was going to reach out and touch her face. Instead, he turned and studied the row of buggies still parked in Leslie's yard.

"So you accept my apology?"

"Sure. *Ya*." She should have stopped there. A warning bell clanged in one portion of her brain. Unfortunately, her mouth wasn't listening to any warning. She simply couldn't resist teasing him just a little. "If you really mean it—mean your apology—maybe you'll let me write you up a business plan."

He turned slowly and met her gaze. "I don't need a business plan. I run a successful business already."

"Yes, but that's what most businesses say until their business is no longer successful and then they wonder why."

"I'm not most businesses."

"So you know what you're going to be doing in five years?"

"No one knows what they're going to be doing in five years."

"Surely you understand what I'm saying. Do you expect to still be installing solar panels on houses and businesses in Shipshe five years from now?"

"Yes. That's what I do."

She should have stopped there, walked away and gone to check on Hannah. But it had been so long since she'd had any real work, work that she loved to do, that her mind had already jogged ahead. "And how many projects did you do last year?"

He quoted a number.

"Your business has grown from the year before?"

"By twenty-seven percent."

She didn't need a calculator, and she'd read just the night before general population and businesses stats on Shipshe.

"Assuming that twenty to twenty-five percent of the population can't or won't add solar panels to their residence or business—"

"They will when they see how well it works."

She didn't answer that. It was a ridiculous statement and they both knew it. There was always a segment of any community that clung to the old ways—whether they were *Englisch* or Amish. "Assuming that seventy-five percent are willing to install, you'll run out of work in six years."

"What?" He looked at her as if she had her *kapp* on crooked.

"It's simple math and analysis."

"Uh-huh."

"Of course, you don't have to listen to me."

"I'm not. This entire conversation is ludicrous."

If he hadn't said that, if he hadn't called her ludicrous, she might have let it be. As it was, she could practically feel steam leaving her ears. "Just keep on... installing... And when you run out of work, I'm sure you'll think of something else to do."

"You've been in town all of ten days, but you know more about the area than I do?"

"Elijah, it's simple math."

"Oh, is it?"

"You're obviously *gut* at what you do."

"You think?"

"But there are only so many homes and businesses. At the rate you're growing, you will run out of work in the next six years."

"Simple math."

"*Ya.* With a business plan, you can anticipate and plan for that."

"Except I don't need a business plan, and I don't want one."

Fortunately Hannah picked that moment to wake up. Her *doschder* might be small, but her lungs were mighty.

Which provided the perfect excuse for Faith to flee the room. Why had she thought Elijah was ready to be reasonable? Just because he'd flashed that charming smile at her didn't mean his attitude had changed.

And as she fed and changed Hannah, she had to admit to herself that it wasn't so unusual for him to resist. Amish notoriously went with the flow. They called it *Gotte's wille*, which was all good and fine, but in regards to business Faith looked at it as poor planning.

All she needed was for a few businesses to give her

a try, and word would get out that what she could provide was useful.

She'd hoped Elijah might be one of those first businesses.

That obviously wasn't going to happen.

Well, she had Leslie. They'd already met twice to discuss how she could begin her bed-and-breakfast. She didn't need Elijah's endorsement, and she certainly wouldn't beg for it.

But it would have been nice.

Two weeks later, Elijah's *mamm* stopped by his place. She brought with her freshly baked bread and a platter of peanut butter bars. Elijah offered to make a pot of coffee, and the next thing he knew they were discussing Faith Yoder as snow fell softly outside his windows on a Friday afternoon.

He casually relayed the conversation they'd had on the work day—the one where Faith had predicted the demise of his business. At least he thought he sounded casual. He'd recovered from his irritation days ago.

"She said that to you?" His *mamm* looked as if she wanted to laugh. Thankfully, she didn't. "She said you'd run out of work in six years?"

"She did."

Instead of seeing how crazy Faith's prediction was, his *mamm* started talking about how intelligent she was and how hard she was working to support herself.

Elijah sipped his coffee and watched the snowfall build up outside the kitchen window.

Two months, at least, until spring.

The winter seemed to stretch endlessly out ahead of him.

"Are you listening to me at all?"

"Of course I am."

"Then tell me what I just said." His *mamm* nudged the Tupperware container toward him.

He stared at a peanut butter bar, and his mind flashed back on an image of Hannah as they'd had their luncheon in the barn. Apparently she'd recently discovered peanut butter, and she had the stuff all over her hands and face. She'd looked like an angel covered in peanut butter.

His *mamm* tapped the table, and he looked up in surprise.

"Son, I can tell that you're plainly smitten with this girl—"

"I am not."

"But there's something you need to consider."

Arguing with his *mamm* was a futile exercise, so he glanced toward the ceiling, praying for patience, then motioned for her to continue.

"Faith has had to be more independent than most women. The fact that she was an only child and learned her father's business started the ball rolling in that direction. Then the situation with her husband—"

"How do you know about that?"

"We had a long conversation after church on Sunday."

"You did?"

"*Ya.* Women confide in one another, Elijah. Don't look so surprised."

He shifted uncomfortably in his chair. "Did she say anything about me?"

"We talked mostly about Hannah, and a little about how she ended up here in Shipshe."

"Oh." It was ridiculous that he felt disappointed. Why would she have talked about him? And why was he acting like a schoolboy with a crush? He was not infatuated with Faith Yoder. The very idea was ridiculous.

"So my point is that the fact that she has a head for business shouldn't come as a surprise. She is carrying a heavy burden. It will be her job to provide for Hannah for the next seventeen years, maybe longer."

"Surely Faith will marry before that."

"Some women don't." His *mamm* sat back, cradling the mug of coffee in her hands. "Sometimes when a woman's been hurt, when she's learned the hard way that life doesn't always turn out as we might expect... as we might hope... Well, it's hard for them to trust again."

Elijah felt a twinge of guilt, though he wasn't sure what he had to feel guilty about. "All that has nothing to do with her bossing me around about my own business." He stuffed half a peanut bar into his mouth.

"So what she said... You disagree with it?"

He stared at the table, picked up another peanut butter bar, then realized he wasn't hungry and dropped it back into the container. "I don't know, *Mamm*. I just work every day, do the best I can and don't worry about the rest."

"*Ya?* That's a *gut* plan spiritually speaking, but business-wise I'm not so sure. Perhaps *Gotte* put Faith in your life for a reason."

"Huh?"

"Maybe you should listen to what she has to say. It never hurts to listen." She cocked her head and waited, and then when he didn't offer an opinion, she added,

"You know, if you employed Faith's services for your business, then others might follow your example and do the same. You're a leader in this community, Elijah, especially in business circles."

"I don't know about being a leader."

"You could still be a good example—point others toward her business."

"I do want to see her be successful."

"Of course you do."

"I just don't think that I personally need her help. I've been running my own business for quite some time."

"Still, it couldn't hurt to listen."

He let out a long sigh. This conversation would end more quickly if he stopped contradicting her. He understood now that she'd obviously come over with an agenda. She wouldn't leave until she had what she'd come for, and apparently that involved extracting a promise from him.

"What do you want me to do?"

"Just schedule an appointment. Let Faith do…whatever it is she does with business plans. You don't have to follow her suggestions."

"Indeed, I don't."

"So you'll call her?"

He drummed his fingers against the table. It wasn't as if it would hurt anything. As his *mamm* had pointed out, he didn't have to take her advice.

"I could do that."

"Gut." She actually clapped her hands. Standing, she walked to the sink and rinsed out her cup. After she'd pulled on her coat, scarf and bonnet, she turned to him and put a hand on each of his shoulders. His

mamm wasn't usually demonstrative about her emotions, but she cocked her head, then kissed his cheek. "And remember to be patient."

"I am patient."

"Don't take that bossy tone you have with her."

"What bossy tone?"

"Treat her like that injured fawn you raised when you were eight. Do you remember that? I never thought you'd have the patience, but you did. It was quite amazing."

And with that, she left.

Women were a mystery to Elijah—didn't matter if it was his *mamm*, his *schweschder* or Faith Yoder. But if it would satisfy his *mamm* and cause her attention to hop over to one of his other siblings, he'd call Faith and make an appointment.

After all, what could possibly go wrong?

Chapter Six

Something told Faith that Elijah might be avoiding her.

At church, he'd made quite the point of staying on the other side of the barn where they held their service, even during the meal and socializing afterward.

And he hadn't been by Leslie's even once to check on the finished room. It just seemed odd after he'd shown such interest in where she would settle. But then again, perhaps he was glad to be rid of her, not that he was responsible in any way. So he had offered her a ride on that cold snowy night at the Mercantile. She had to smile when she considered how she must have looked—like a lost orphan.

She slapped her dusting cloth against the desk where she did her accounting work, banishing the dust with renewed vigor.

She wasn't lost.

And she wasn't an orphan—well, she was but that was beside the point.

She certainly didn't care if Elijah was avoiding her.

So it was that you could have knocked Faith over with a clean nappie when she checked the phone shack and had a call from Elijah—not just any call, but apparently he wanted to make an appointment to discuss his business.

Something suspicious was going on.

She knew for a fact that the last thing Elijah wanted was her advice. Then again, maybe he'd thought about what she'd said and come to his senses.

She called him back at his phone shack's number and left a message telling him what items she'd need to see and that he could bring them over anytime.

It was almost as if he was waiting for her to leave, because he brought the accounting records over the one time she went to town with Hannah. She hadn't taken Hannah to a doctor since moving to Shipshe, and she wanted to stay current on both her *doschder*'s inoculations and well visits. Some Amish didn't. Some said such things were a waste of time and money, but she knew better. She'd suffered enough from such old-fashioned thinking.

Nein. Hannah would have whatever medical care she needed.

The doctor pronounced Hannah as healthy as a newborn lamb, and gave Faith some literature on one-year-olds.

By the time she arrived back at Leslie's, Elijah's accounting books were waiting for her. Later that night, she dived into her analysis.

It took her three days to properly go over his books, do some research at the library and combine it all into a business plan. Before she'd had Hannah, she could have done it in half that time, but she didn't resent having to stop and feed or bathe or play with her *doschder*.

Hannah was the joy of her life, and if it meant work took twice as long then so be it.

Faith was quite aware that in the blink of an eye her little girl would be going to school, and she'd have all day to work. Before she knew it, Hannah would be dating, then marrying, and she'd be alone with all the time in the world. She was having just such dark thoughts when Leslie walked into the room.

"What happened?"

"Happened?"

"You look as if you've been crying."

"Maybe a little." Faith felt foolish. She used a corner of her apron to dry her eyes. "I was just thinking of how fast it all goes, how Hannah will be grown and moved away in no time at all."

Leslie smiled and sank into the chair across from her. "Mommy blues."

"Huh?"

"You have mommy blues. Most everyone gets them at one time or the other."

"Did you?" Since moving in nearly a month before, Faith had met all of Leslie's family. They were a boisterous, loving group, and it was easy enough to imagine Leslie as a young mother. But a mom who cried in the middle of the day for no reason? That was harder to imagine.

"Indeed, I did. Seems like it was worse after my second and…" She drummed her fingers against the table and stared up at the ceiling. "Sixth. Those were the hard ones."

"Why don't you live with one of your children, Leslie? I've met them all, and they're perfectly nice people."

Leslie laughed. "You're right about that, but still... I'm not quite ready to give up this dream that John and I had."

"I'm excited about your business."

"As am I. Did I tell you I scheduled David Lapp to start building as soon as the weather clears?"

"Have I met him?"

"*Nein.* He specializes in tiny houses for *Englischers*, but he attends the other church district here in Shipshe."

"So all we need is for the snow to stop."

"*Ya.* That would be *gut*. David said not to worry. He said once the weather clears, he can work pretty quickly."

They spoke about plans to create a B and B from tiny houses scattered around her property. Faith hoped they'd turned away from the topic of mommy blues, but when she stood to go and check on Hannah, Leslie stopped her with a hand on her arm.

"You're done with Elijah's business plan?"

"*Ya.* I am. I only need to go to the phone shack and tell him to come and pick it up."

"Tomorrow the weather is supposed to be better, and there are some things I could use from town. Why don't you meet him at the coffee shop while you're there?"

It sounded like a setup to Faith, but Leslie had done so much for her that she didn't have the heart to say no. So when the snowfall let up later that afternoon, she bundled up in her coat and walked down the road to the phone shack. February and still no sign of spring. Well, what did she expect? Flowers to pop out of the snow?

She didn't know if it was leaving the message for Elijah, having some time outside or looking forward to a few hours in town, but she did feel better as she walked back toward home.

Home.

It was a funny word to use for someplace she'd lived only a month, but Leslie's place felt like the spot they were supposed to be. It was safe, and more than that Leslie's house was where Hannah could thrive— a place filled with love. So she felt a little lonely. And yes, at times she wondered about her own future and the things she'd lost. She desperately missed her husband. She longed for the feel of a man's arms around her, sharing an early morning coffee, talking about their day together. She wondered if *Gotte* had that in mind for her, or perhaps she was meant to be a single *mamm* for the rest of her life.

Regardless, she was grateful for what she had.

As for the loneliness, she'd do what she'd done since Jonas's death—she'd push it down inside and pretend it wasn't there.

Elijah walked into the coffee shop the next morning, ten minutes later than they had agreed. He hurried over to where Faith was waiting.

"Sorry. Boots first didn't want to take the harness, and then when he did… Let's just say my gelding thought he should be in charge of our route."

Faith chuckled. "It is a beautiful morning to play in the snow."

"Boots agrees with you."

Elijah thought Faith looked exceptionally pretty. There was color in her cheeks, and if he wasn't mistaken she was wearing a new frock. He mentally slapped his forehead. How would he know if her dress was new or not? More than likely it was from the bags of clothes that folks had given to her on the work day. He couldn't bring that up, and so he supposed complimenting her was out of the question.

"Problem?" She watched him, waiting.

"Only that I've never seen you wear that color of blue before. It looks *gut* on you."

"Oh." Her cheeks blushed an even darker shade of pink, but she murmured *"danki"* before glancing away.

"Let me grab some coffee. Would you like anything?"

"Sure. Decaf coffee with whipped cream on top."

"Think I'll order the same, only I need mine caffeinated."

She had to move the stack of folders to an adjacent chair when he came back. He'd also purchased a cinnamon pretzel roll, a blueberry muffin and a croissant, since he hadn't known what she liked.

"Hungry?"

"Yes, but I didn't buy it all for me."

"Oh…"

"Not hungry?"

"Actually I'm starved. That was very kind of you."

Once they had divided up the food, he asked how Hannah was doing.

"Gut." She seemed surprised that he'd asked.

"She reminds me of my oldest niece—when she was a *boppli*." He stared out the window, then looked at her and wiggled his eyebrows. "She's driving a buggy now, and don't ask me how that happened. They grow up fast."

"Funny you should say that. It's exactly what I was brooding over yesterday."

They spent the next fifteen minutes talking about how days could go so slow but the years seemed to fly by.

"I thought Jonas and I would have at least fifty years together." Faith stared down at her half of the cinnamon pretzel, then met his gaze and shrugged. "Life doesn't always turn out the way we expect."

Which exactly mirrored what his *mamm* had said. Elijah pushed away the food, crossed his arms on the table and looked directly at Faith. "You've never mentioned how he died."

When she hesitated, he added, "Of course, if you don't want to talk about it…"

"*Nein.* It's just, well, people don't ask. I guess they're afraid it will upset me, but sometimes it seems like Jonas didn't exist. I look at Hannah, and I know he did. I remember, though, and sometimes I'm afraid that if I don't ever talk about him that I'll forget."

"It must be hard."

"It is, though it's been almost two years now. I was in my first trimester with Hannah when he died."

"What happened?"

"Sleep apnea."

Elijah almost choked on the sip of coffee he'd swallowed. "I didn't know you could die from that."

"It weakens the heart."

"Wow."

"The most difficult part of it was that we knew that he had the condition. I'd wake and hear him stop breathing, or it seemed like it. Perhaps it was only a long pause. He went to the doctor, and the doctor told him it was important to get a CPAP machine."

"I've heard of those. Not many Amish have them."

"Right. And Jonas's dad, well… I think I've already told you about him."

"You did, but what does that have to do with this?"

"He said it was a waste of money, said until Jonas was living on his own, supporting his own family, he wouldn't be wasting money on *Englisch* gadgets." She broke off a piece of the pretzel, but left it on her napkin. "He died two weeks after the doctor's appointment. We were… We had made plans to move out on our own, but we didn't move fast enough."

"His death wasn't your fault, Faith."

"I know that." She nodded emphatically, picked up the piece of pretzel and popped it in her mouth. "I know that now. I met with my bishop regularly after that—working through my anger and grief. Some days, though… It's still hard."

She cleared her throat and focused on folding the napkin in front of her.

"You miss him."

"I do, though in truth now I realize that we barely knew one another. It's just that raising Hannah alone… I worry about her." She sat up straighter, pushed aside the coffee and food and grabbed a folder off the top stack. "But we didn't come here to talk about my problems. Let's discuss your business."

Perhaps it was the fact that she'd lowered her guard and shared her heart with him, but Elijah found himself really listening to her business ideas for the first time. He wasn't too proud to admit that what she laid out for him over the next half hour made sense.

"You want me to expand my business to Goshen?"

"Or Middlebury. *Ya.* I think it would be a *gut* idea."

"I wouldn't know where to start."

She rifled through his folders and pulled out an employment sheet. "I think you start here."

"What does Mose have to do with it?"

"He's a *gut* employee?"

"*Ya*. He's been with me the longest."

"But he lives in Goshen."

"He does. His cousin is a Mennonite and gives him a ride to whatever work site we're at."

"Don't you see? He's in Goshen and you're in Shipshe. He could supervise the Goshen work, and you could both split the work in Middlebury. This would triple your market. You'd have enough work to last at least ten more years."

"Wow."

Faith sat back, a smile brightening her face. "So you'll consider it?"

"I will, and I'll talk to Mose."

"There's one other thing."

Elijah sat back and pretended to be completely put out. "There always is one more thing with women."

"Uh-huh. I think you should approach Old Eli about providing solar panels to the schools."

"The schools?"

"Sure. Why not?"

"Who would pay for them?"

"It could come out of the benevolence fund."

"I don't know about that."

"Or maybe parents whose children attend the schools would be willing to split the cost."

"That's a possibility."

Faith leaned forward and tapped the stack of folders they'd gone through. "There are twenty-three schools in the Shipshe/Middlebury/Goshen area."

"That's a lot of schools."

"Indeed it is."

Elijah had been hunched down in his chair, but now he sat up straight. "Why not? I'll talk to Old Eli about it."

Together they bussed the table, and as they walked out of the coffee shop, he asked her about Leslie.

"She's doing *gut*."

"You've done a business plan for her?"

"I have."

"And?"

"I suppose it's no secret. She's going to have David Lapp build six tiny houses on her property. She'll space them out in a semicircle around the meadow to her east, starting with the building pads she already had done."

"Wow."

"I know. Right?"

"Why mini-houses?"

"*Englischers* like their privacy, but they also want to experience the simplicity and minimalism of Amish life. It's a nice compromise."

He understood then what the thing was that Faith possessed, the thing that helped her be so *gut* at writing business plans. She could envision the future, and she could understand what other people needed. That's what business was, after all, meeting the needs of people.

He walked her to Leslie's buggy. After she'd climbed in, he said, "*Danki* for telling me about Jonas."

"I appreciate your asking and listening."

"It could be that I'm being bold, or maybe it's all the caffeine talking, but I think I know what you and I need."

Faith's eyes widened in surprise.

"A *gut* friend."

"*Ya*. You might be right about that."

And beginning that afternoon, that's what Elijah vowed to be—a *gut* friend. Over the next two months, he visited Leslie's place often, took small gifts to Hannah and generally made a nuisance of himself. No one seemed to mind.

Through February and into March, he spent at least two nights a week playing Dutch Blitz with Faith and Leslie.

When sweet little Hannah contracted the flu in late March and had to be hospitalized, he was at the hospital almost as much as Faith.

And gradually she began to relax around him.

Hannah began babbling whenever he walked into the room, though she'd yet to say his name. He understood then what had been missing from his life, and the length he was willing to go in order to readjust his priorities.

Elijah wasn't blind to what was happening.

He was falling in love with both Faith and Hannah, but he was determined to give her time, to let her work through her grief and establish her business.

After all, there was really no need to rush things. It wasn't as if she was going to move anywhere. Or so he told himself.

Chapter Seven

The day was brisk and the sunshine bright though there were clouds building in the west. Hadn't Leslie said the temperature was supposed to rise to nearly sixty? A real rarity in early April, but she'd also said snow was scheduled for the end of the week. Faith couldn't stand sitting inside and looking at ledgers and numbers for another minute. Leslie had gone to town for supplies, and Hannah was playing in her pen.

"How about we go for a walk, baby girl?"

She didn't know if Hannah understood what she'd said, but she looked up at Faith and held out the toy she'd been chewing on. "Yup. Daisy Duck can go with us. Let's get your sweater and *kapp* on. There's a bit of wind outside today."

Ten minutes later, they were walking around the property.

The sunshine raised her spirits, and the row of tiny houses made her smile. Leslie would be ready to accept reservations at her B and B by May. Faith was predicting a long and successful business.

"Do we go or stay, Hannah girl?"

Hannah didn't answer, but she did point down the lane and shout "Boos. Boos."

Sure enough, Eli was driving Boots toward the main house. When she waved at him, he angled toward where they were standing next to the second tiny house.

"Whoa." He pulled up on Boots's reins, and Hannah let out a squeal. Hopping out of the buggy, he walked over to where they stood. "Someone's happy to see me."

"Boos!"

"She's happy to see your horse."

"So you say." Elijah smiled as Hannah practically jumped into his arms. "I'm going to pretend she's happy to see me, but take her to see Boots before she bounces out of my arms."

"She definitely adores that horse."

"What's not to like?"

Boots tossed his head in agreement.

Faith stood on the tiny house's porch, watching the three of them—her *doschder*, her friend and a feisty chestnut gelding with white socks. They were doing well in Shipshe. Hannah was happy, and Faith was settled. It was true, life hadn't turned out quite like she'd imagined it when she was a *youngie*, but it wasn't bad. She was so grateful for her little girl and for a safe place to live.

But there was the letter to consider.

It was her job to prayerfully consider all possible options. Wasn't it?

"Is something wrong?"

She hadn't noticed that Elijah had walked back over and was standing in front of her. He stood there, holding Hannah in his arms and moving his head back and forth as her *doschder* reached for his hat. He waited, patiently, for her to tire of the game. That was one thing she'd learned that had surprised her—Elijah was an exceedingly patient man when he decided to be.

Plopping down onto the porch steps, she shrugged. She honestly didn't know how to broach the subject of her moving. It was all so sudden.

"Best to jump in if you don't know where to start. Unless it's private, that is."

"Not private. I value your opinion."

"You do?"

"Certainly."

"What about the time I suggested you start quilting for a living?"

"Not your fault. You'd never seen me quilt."

Elijah sat beside her, still holding Hannah, who was now playing with the toy he'd pulled out of his pocket. He was always bringing her something—a flower or treat or toy. Elijah King would make a fine father when he found the right woman and settled down. She'd once thought he had feelings for her, but then something had happened. He'd pulled back and their relationship had taken on a more friendly tone.

And yet sometimes she caught him looking at her in a way that sent her pulse racing and her mind jumping to conclusions.

"You're not that bad a quilter."

"I'm not that good."

"The buggy quilt you gave me is something I'll always treasure."

"One of the squares is upside down."

"True."

"Another is sideways."

"I hardly noticed."

"Three times I stuck my finger and smeared blood on the fabric. When I tried to wash it out, the colors bled."

"So that's what happened. I'd wondered."

Discussing her missteps in quilting helped to ease the tension in her shoulders. And though she valued Leslie's opinion, Elijah was just the person she needed to talk to about this. He understood what it was like to be a young adult in today's world. He understood that their lives and decisions were different from what the generation before them had lived through. Perhaps it was that way for every generation.

She only knew that the choices facing her seemed difficult.

How was one to know what the best thing was?

What if she chose wrong and regretted it the rest of her life?

She glanced again at Elijah and plunged in. "I received a letter yesterday…from Sugarcreek."

"Where you lived before—with your parents."

"Yes."

"But I thought you don't have any family there."

"Correct. This letter was from a friend of my *dat*'s."

Faith picked at her thumbnail, wondering where to begin. She glanced out at Leslie's farm. It was a fine day in April. No doubt, Elijah had places to be. She best get on with it if she wanted his opinion.

"He'd heard of my situation…heard of it some time ago. He'd sent a letter to my in-laws last fall."

"Let me guess. You never received it." A hint of anger colored Elijah's voice.

"Correct. I never received it. Levi didn't realize at

first that I hadn't, so he tried again, waited some time and finally contacted the bishop, who sent him my new address."

"This Levi… He was a *gut* friend of your *dat*'s?"

"He was. I spent many a Sunday afternoon at his home." Faith smiled at the memory from before her life had become so complicated, from before her mistakes. Then she glanced over at Hannah and suddenly felt the need to hold the child in her arms. She pulled her into her lap.

"Levi had heard about my troubles, and he offered for me to come and live with them. He said that many of the local businesses had asked about me and that he thought I could start back up where I left off."

"Creating business plans."

"Ya."

"Which would mean less accounting work."

"Exactly."

"Less peering at numbers and working with spreadsheets." Elijah gave a mock shudder. When Faith didn't respond, he bumped his shoulder against hers. "It's *gut* to hear from old friends. Why is this bothering you?"

"Because I'm wondering if I should move."

"Oh."

"You were listening, right?"

"Ya. I was. Only I guess I didn't want to hear that part so I skipped right over it."

Since Hannah had started walking, she was rarely happy in her mother's lap for long. She arched her back and pushed away, then loudly proclaimed, "Down."

Faith placed her on the ground. She held on to the porch floor, which was only a foot off the ground, then proceeded to use it to scoot down the length of the porch, looking back and laughing at her mother.

"She's growing so fast," Elijah said.

"You think so, too? Seems to me that she was just learning to roll over and now look at her."

"So you think you should consider this offer?"

"I have *freinden* in Ohio. I pulled away from them, when I met Jonas, but they're people I grew up with. I know they'd support me. They'd be kind."

"Why didn't you…" Elijah stopped abruptly and shook his head once.

"Go ahead and ask it. You've never held back before." She couldn't quite meet his gaze. She suspected she knew what he was going to ask, and it was something that had troubled her since receiving the letter.

"Why didn't you go back to Ohio when you knew you needed to leave Adams County?"

"I suppose I thought we needed a fresh start. Plus, I think sometimes it's harder to go back to where people know you—even if they're kind people. They saw your mistakes, your missteps. You'll always be the girl who messed up, moved away, then came back."

Elijah crossed his arms. "The way you say it makes it sound as if what happened was your fault."

"If you look at it a certain way, it was."

"I don't see that."

"Really? I shouldn't have agreed to marry Jonas without meeting his family. I should have courted longer. I was grieving the death of my parents, and I was scared, but that doesn't account for my lack of judgment."

"You couldn't have known, Faith."

He reached out and squeezed her hand, causing butterflies to jump and tumble in her stomach.

"I should have known, though. I should have at least considered that it wouldn't be the rosy picture I'd painted in my head." She stood, retrieved Hannah from the end of the porch and put her in front of Elijah. Hannah held on to Elijah's knees, then lunged to the right, giggling and moving right then left as if she was ready for a game of tag.

"Let's try to focus on the present. Do you want to move to Ohio?"

"I don't know."

"Do you think you'd be happier there?"

"Who can say?"

"But the work would be better."

"Yes, maybe. I mean things are going well here, and I've even had a few people come to me for a business plan."

"That's *wunderbaar*."

"It's a start. The bulk of my work is still accounting, which you know…"

"Isn't your favorite thing. You mentioned as much."

Hannah plopped to the ground and began to rub her eyes.

"Baby girl looks sleepy."

"She needs lunch. Can you stay?"

"Of course."

So they moved into Leslie's kitchen—the one with all the sunlight and the butter-yellow paint. Faith remembered the first morning she'd come there. She remembered Elijah's confusion when she'd explained what she did for a living. It seemed that he'd grown to accept her now, and Faith knew that he cared for Hannah.

He was a *gut* friend.

She would miss him if she left.

She realized in a moment of clarity that she was afraid to admit her feelings for Elijah—even to herself. If she allowed herself to care for him, if she allowed herself to love again, could she withstand being hurt? Because few things in life were ever a certainty. She was wiser than the young woman who had married Jonas.

"This place feels like home," she said as she cut up a banana for Hannah, then placed it on the tray of the high chair.

Elijah was making a peanut butter and jam sandwich, carefully cutting it into small triangles that Hannah could manage. Faith looked at him, really looked at him, for the first time in a long while. Was there a spark between them? Did she want more from their relationship? Was she even ready for that?

The questions filled her mind, collided with the contents of Levi's letter and made her wish she could take a nap. She supposed the real question she didn't want to face was whether her relationship with Elijah might change into something else.

Was that what she wanted?

Was it what he wanted?

And was it relevant at all in light of the offer to move to Ohio?

As if he could read her thoughts, Elijah raised his gaze to meet hers. He stepped closer, still holding the plate of peanut butter triangles.

"I would never try to tell you what to do, Faith.

You're an intelligent woman and a *gut mamm*. I know you can figure this out…"

"But?"

"But the truth is…" He stepped even closer, put his right hand under her chin, then leaned forward and kissed her lightly on the lips. "The truth is that I don't want you to go."

Elijah was stunned at his own boldness. He'd told himself that he wasn't going to push Faith. That he was going to be patient and wait until she sent the right signals.

But would he even recognize those?

And could he afford to wait?

He wasn't willing to take that chance.

Faith's cheeks blushed a lovely pink, and he longed to take her in his arms. Of course, at that moment, Hannah began impatiently beating her plastic spoon against her tray.

"Patience isn't her gift."

"Maybe she'll grow into it."

"Something tells me she might not." Faith took the plate from him and placed it in front of Hannah. She sat down in the chair next to her *doschder* and covered her face with her hands.

"Hey. It's not that bad." Elijah sat beside her, pulled her hands down and away, covered them with his. "I won't kiss you anymore if it's that upsetting."

She glanced up at him and shook her head. "It wasn't the kiss, Elijah."

"It wasn't?"

"Nein."

Before she could say anything else, he leaned forward and kissed her again. He thought Faith's lips were the sweetest thing he'd ever encountered. They pulled apart, both glancing at Hannah, who appeared too mesmerized by her sandwich to pay them any mind.

He cleared his throat, which was suddenly tight with hope and love and the possibility of all that might be. "We won't get away with this when she's older."

"This?"

"Making out."

"Elijah King. I was not making out with you."

"But you wanted to."

A smile replaced her worried expression, which was what he wanted—what he needed—to see.

"I don't know what to do, Elijah."

He turned her hand over, traced the inside of her palm with his fingertip. "I can't tell you what's best. I think you need to carefully consider what this friend of your *dat* has offered and pray on it…which I'm sure you've done."

"I have."

"And talk to Leslie."

"She doesn't want me to go, but says she understands if I decide to. She… She's become like a *mammi* to Hannah."

"I can't tell you what is the best path for your life," he repeated. His heart beat faster now, and he could feel sweat pooling down his back. Best to jump in and say what was on his heart. He'd never forgive himself if this was the moment and he missed it. Better to know—even if the knowing meant that the dream he'd treasured these past few months was shattered.

"I can tell you that I want you to stay. I want you here, Faith. I care about you and Hannah."

"You've been a *gut* friend."

"I want to be more than a friend."

There. He'd said it! He'd planned on waiting until summer, maybe fall, but then life didn't always give you the option of waiting.

Faith was worrying her bottom lip, which seemed to be a bad sign.

But then she glanced up at him and smiled.

"I would like that," she admitted.

"Yes!" He jumped out of his chair, clasped his hands together and raised them over his head in victory. Then he remembered he was an adult, and he sat back down. "I was worried that you only saw me as a *bruder*."

"And I was worried you'd begun courting, maybe someone without so much baggage."

"I love your baggage." He glanced at Hannah, who now had peanut butter and jam smeared all over her face.

Faith's expression slipped into something more somber. "I can't…can't make a mistake again. Not now. Not with Hannah."

"I won't be a mistake."

"I thought the same was true of Jonas."

Elijah sighed. He'd known this would be the hard part. His *mamm* had cautioned him that a woman who'd been hurt needed time to trust again.

"You've met my family. You know they're nothing like your in-laws. You know my family and our community are both made up of *gut* people who care for you and for Hannah." He waited for her to raise her eyes to his—those lovely brown eyes that he sometimes saw in his dreams. "We'll move slowly. You can take all the time you need."

Faith nodded as if she heard, but her thoughts seemed a thousand miles away. She stood, extracted Hannah from her high chair and walked to the sink to wash her face and hands.

Elijah handed her a towel when she was done.

"Look at that." Faith nodded at the scene outside the window, toward the west where a rainbow arched the sky.

"Must have rained over in Middlebury."

"And to think we could have snow in a few days."

"It won't be much—winter's last hurrah before spring sends it packing."

They walked out onto the porch. Faith stood there, holding a now-sleepy baby Hannah in her arms, and Elijah stood beside her. The rainbow lingered on the horizon, offering promises and hope and *gut* things from above.

"*Gotte*'s promise, right?" Elijah slipped his arm around her waist, pulled her closer against his side. She felt perfect there, as if *Gotte* had made her to be the other half of him.

"*Ya.*"

"Like the good book says, He's promising us that He cares for us and is providing for us."

"I like to think so."

"This friend of your *dat*'s… You can write him and tell him that you'd like to give your life here some time. Ask him if it's a standing offer."

She looked up into his eyes, and Elijah felt his pulse jump again. If he was going to get used to dating Faith Yoder, he'd have to learn to deal with her closeness without having a heart attack.

"It's a *gut* idea."

"In the meantime I'll work on wooing you over to life in Shipshewana."

She reached up, touched his face, then stood on tiptoe and kissed him softly. "I'd like that even better."

Epilogue

Five years later

Faith put a clean shirt on baby Joseph, checked that she had everything she could possibly need in the diaper bag, then hurried out to the buggy.

Hannah was riding next to Elijah, holding Boots's reins. "Look, *Mamm*. I'm driving."

"Indeed you are. Now scoot in the back next to your *bruder*."

Nathan had recently turned three. He glanced up at the sound of his name, even as he stuffed something in his pocket.

"What do you have there, Nathan?"

"Something."

"Is it something that jumps?"

"Sometimes."

Faith nudged Elijah as she scooted next to him on the buggy seat. She liked sitting next to her husband. She liked riding with him with the children tucked around them. It reminded her of all that *Gotte* had provided in so short a time.

"Your son has a critter in his pocket again."

"Ya?"

"You probably helped him catch it."

"That might or might not be true, but if we stop to deal with it, we'll be late to Leslie's."

Faith shook her head in mock exasperation, then glanced back at Hannah and Nathan. Their heads were touching as they both huddled over whatever he was holding.

Finally she yielded. "As long as it's not a snake."

"Definitely not a snake. After that last one, the harmless garden snake that almost caused you to faint, we had a heart-to-heart about gals and snakes."

"Gals don't like snakes!" Nathan proclaimed.

"I do. I like snakes." Hannah scooted to the front of her seat, putting one small hand on each parent. *"Aenti* Leslie does, too. She told me that all creatures are *gut."*

"True, but some need to be viewed from a distance." Faith was reminded of the large spider her son had brought into the kitchen the week before.

"Like bears," Hannah proclaimed.

"And lions!" Nathan shouted. Just when you thought Nathan wasn't listening, he jumped in with an exuberant comment.

"Looking forward to the afternoon?" Elijah asked.

"I am. Leslie has a full group staying in her tiny houses this week."

"They like hearing from you about Amish businesses. They're always surprised to learn that many of us do things in addition to farming."

"Like installing solar panels?" she said, smiling.

He smiled back. *"Ya.* Like that."

They'd been speaking to Leslie's guests for about

a year. Each week on Thursday afternoon, they made their way over to her place for a luncheon and discussion. The questions always made Faith laugh.

Were women allowed to work? *All mothers work, all the time.*

Did their clothes have buttons? *Yes!*

What was it like to raise a large family without the conveniences of modern living? *She didn't have a large family yet, but when she did she would let them know.*

She studied her husband, and a small laugh escaped her lips.

"What? Hay in my hair again?"

He combed his fingers through his hair, then asked Hannah to pass him his hat.

"Just thinking of how happy I am."

"I'm happy, *Mamm*," Hannah chimed in, while she sat back to examine whatever Nathan was sheltering.

"I'm happy, too, and so is my frog." Nathan's voice was soft, low, full of wonder.

There was complete silence in the buggy as Faith closed her eyes and prayed for patience. Elijah squeezed her hand, then leaned over and kissed her.

"Ew," Hannah and Nathan said together.

"They're always watching," she murmured.

"Fine by me. It's *gut* for them to see that their *dat* loves their *mamm*."

"But kissing is mushy," Hannah protested.

"I would kiss a frog," Nathan said. "If it would let me."

Elijah wiggled his eyebrows at her and ran his fingers through his beard. It had begun to gray in the past year, which Faith found quite attractive. She liked to tease him about it. He was only thirty-seven, but he said his *dat* had grayed early, too. *Daddi* Joe, as the children called him, was a dear man whom Faith had learned to love. He was as gentle with the children as a *mamm* was with a newborn. It had been Faith's idea to name their second son after him. In many ways, *Daddi* Joe had restored her faith in people again, in families.

As they pulled into Leslie's place, Faith looked out over the tiny houses—an even dozen—and remembered when she'd first come to meet with Leslie. She didn't know then that *Gotte* was providing a dear friend, someone who could stand in the place of her mother. No one would ever replace her *mamm*, and Faith didn't think *Gotte* worked that way. He didn't take away one person and replace him or her with another. People weren't replaceable. But she did believe that *Gotte* sought to fill the holes in their lives with new friends and relationships and loved ones.

She glanced at Elijah.

Remembered Jonas.

Nein. Gotte's ways weren't her ways, but He was *gut*. That she was convinced of. As her little family climbed out of the buggy and walked toward the waiting group of *Englischers*, that was the single thought on Faith's mind—*Gotte*'s abiding goodness.

* * * * *

If you loved this story,
pick up the other books in the
Indiana Amish Brides series,

A Widow's Hope
Amish Christmas Memories
A Perfect Amish Match
The Amish Christmas Matchmaker
An Unlikely Amish Match
The Amish Christmas Secret

from bestselling author
Vannetta Chapman

Available now from Love Inspired!

Find more great reads at www.LoveInspired.com

Dear Reader,

Have you ever been afraid of making a decision?

Faith Yoder has made some choices that weren't very well thought-out. The result is a child whom she loves desperately, and a life that is terribly hard. Faith is paralyzed by the idea that she will decide something that will make their life even worse.

Elijah King is all confidence. He's financially successful and well respected in the community. He's also lonely. How did he miss out on the most important things in life—family and love? With typical self-assurance, he forges ahead at full speed—certain that God will provide the perfect wife to walk by his side and create the perfect family.

Then Elijah meets Faith. She's lost and very strong-willed. He sympathizes with the troubles that she's endured, and he believes Hannah to be the most adorable child in Shipshewana, Indiana. But why does Faith have to be a business planner?

Faith and Elijah have taken drastically different paths in life, and yet God has brought them together at this moment to befriend one another.

I hope you enjoyed reading *Stranded in the Snow*. I welcome comments and letters at vannettachapman@gmail.com.

May we continue to "always give thanks to God the Father for everything, in the name of our Lord Jesus Christ" (Ephesians 5:20).

Blessings,
Vannetta

CARING FOR THE AMISH BABY

Carrie Lighte

For my family, who has seen me through many seasons, and my readers, who have made writing Amish romance novels so rewarding.

To every thing there is a season, and a time to every purpose under the heaven: A time to be born, and a time to die; a time to plant, and a time to pluck up that which is planted; A time to kill, and a time to heal; a time to break down, and a time to build up; A time to weep, and a time to laugh; a time to mourn, and a time to dance; A time to cast away stones, and a time to gather stones together; a time to embrace, and a time to refrain from embracing; A time to get, and a time to lose; a time to keep, and a time to cast away; Λ time to rend, and a time to sew; a time to keep silence, and a time to speak; A time to love, and a time to hate; a time of war, and a time of peace.

—*Ecclesiastes* 3:1–8

Chapter One

Leah Zehr clipped her seat belt buckle into place and waved to her niece, nephew and sister-in-law Catherine as the van pulled down the driveway. Catherine was frowning but Leah could hardly contain her glee. One month. She would be gone for one marvelous month.

One month and four days, to be exact. From today, January 28, until she returned on March 2, Leah wouldn't have to take care of any children. She wouldn't have to cook for anyone other than herself, nor would she have to clean up after anyone else. And she definitely wouldn't be tromping across the lawn in the snow to hang any laundry on the clothesline. That's because she was headed from her hometown of Bensonville in Geauga County, Ohio, to the Amish community in Pinecraft, Florida, and the last time it snowed in that part of the country was in the 1970s.

Leah's elderly second cousin, Betty, who lived in Lancaster County, had paid in advance to rent a bungalow for the month of February. Betty had intended to share the house with her three sisters-in-law, but one of them had slipped on the ice and broken her hip, so Betty gifted Leah with the vacation since the two-bedroom bungalow could accommodate up to four people. Betty had a full itinerary planned for her sisters-in-law and herself and she said Leah was welcome to join them, but they understood if she'd rather socialize with "the younger folk."

Other than keeping her half of the bedroom tidy and washing her own dishes, Leah was free to do whatever she wanted. And what she wanted to do was lounge in the sunshine, reading one of the many books she started but never seemed to have time to finish. She also intended to learn to play shuffleboard. And to go bicycling every day.

Most of all, she couldn't wait to visit Siesta Key, the beach she'd heard so much about from those members of her district who were fortunate enough to go there, or who had relatives who went. Leah had never even been to Lake Erie, which was some fifty miles from where she lived, so going to the Gulf of Mexico was more than a dream come true; it was a dream she hadn't even imagined for herself.

"It must be nice to be able to leave town for a month without a care in the world," Catherine had said when Leah told her about her plans. "But when you have two *kinner* to raise, with another one on the way, you have to put your *familye* first."

Leah had been rankled by Catherine's insinuation that she was selfish. *I already know full well that raising children means putting their needs first*, she thought.

She knew because she had practically raised her younger brother and two younger sisters after her parents were killed in a carbon monoxide poisoning accident when she was fifteen. Although Leah's grandparents had assumed guardianship of all four children, they were both older and in ill health, so Leah wound up taking care of them, as well as her siblings. By the time she was nineteen, Leah's grandparents had both died and she was left entirely on her own to finish bringing up her brother and sisters, aged twelve, nine and seven, respectively.

Now that her youngest sister, the last sibling to marry, had gone to live with her in-laws until her husband could build a house in the spring, Leah was alone with Catherine, Leah's brother, Paul, and their two little children. Ever since Catherine had moved into the Zehr family home when she wed Paul five years ago, Leah felt her role as the woman of the house had been usurped by her sister-in-law, who wanted everything done her way, from where to plant the flowers to how to hang the laundry to what to serve when they hosted church—and everything in between. Now that both of Leah's sisters were gone, Leah didn't have anyone to back her up when she asserted herself. Since Paul sided with his wife, Catherine always got her way, but Leah wasn't about to let her sister-in-law pressure her into forgoing this once-in-a-lifetime trip.

"I've never been on a vacation," Leah had pointed out. "You and Paul already got to go to Pinecraft."

Although romantic honeymoons weren't commonplace among the Amish, Pinecraft's popularity had increased over the past two decades, and more and more young couples were going there following their weddings. Older Amish and Mennonite retirees also visited the little Sarasota community in the winter in order to escape the harsh northern climates.

"*Jah*, but that's different. We were on our honey-moon."

"So I'm not allowed to enjoy traveling just because I'm an old maid, is that it?"

Leah was asking the question tongue in cheek; at thirty-four, she didn't consider herself old. And she was single by choice. She'd had her share of men vying to court her over the years, but they were all widow-ers with children of their own and Leah couldn't see how adding more children to their household would help matters. She'd already been struggling to take care of her siblings, and later, to help Catherine with her babies.

Fortunately, their family home was already paid for, so between the quilts and baked goods Leah and her sisters made and sold, as well as the income her brother earned when he began working in a nearby manufacturing plant, the Zehrs hadn't suffered finan-cially. They weren't wealthy by any stretch, but the Lord had always provided for their material needs, otherwise Leah might have felt more pressured to get married.

Her church community and friends had anticipated that once Leah's siblings were teenagers or had moved out of the house, Leah would accept a suitor, but the fact was, she wanted a suitor even less now than she did when she was raising her brother and sisters. Why court if she had no intention of getting married? And why get married when she felt as if she'd already *been* married?

Or at least, she'd felt that she'd already had the major life experiences most Amish people have when they get married; she'd had her own home to run, children to care for and finances to manage. Admittedly, she hadn't experienced what it was like to fall in love and to have a man fall in love with her. But she'd made it this long in her life without a husband, so why did she need one now? Husbands and marriage usually led to babies, and there was no way Leah wanted to go through raising children again.

In fact, she had actually daydreamed about staying in Florida permanently, wondering if it was possible to sell her share of the family house to her brother and find somewhere to live and work in Pinecraft year-round.

I can just imagine what Catherine would have to say about that, she thought. Her brother and sisters wouldn't be very pleased at the idea of her moving so far away, either. And she'd miss them terribly, too. But what would her life be like if she stayed in her family home in Ohio? *I'll probably end up playing nanny to my great-great-nieces and -nephews and catering to Catherine's demands until I'm ninety!*

It wasn't that Leah didn't want to be involved in her nieces' and nephews' lives. Nor was it that she intended to shirk her family obligations—on the contrary, she derived a great deal of satisfaction from her role as a sister and an aunt, as well as from being a member of her church district. But lately she'd felt so restless. As if the time was ripe for a change. She'd asked God to give her a spirit of contentment, but more and more often, she felt as if the Lord was preparing her to do something different.

So she'd been praying about an opportunity in Florida and if God opened the right doors, she'd walk through them. But for now, she was going to appreciate every moment of her month away.

Her first stop was to spend three days with Esther, her closest friend from childhood. Esther had moved from Bensonville to a little town in Holmes County, Ohio, called Fawn Crossing when she married Gabriel Rocke, a wheat and oats farmer, some ten years ago.

After years of trying unsuccessfully to conceive and then suffering two miscarriages, Esther had finally given birth to a girl, Rebekah, who was now six months old. Although Leah never longed for children of her own, she was delighted the Lord had blessed Esther with the desire of her heart and she couldn't wait to spend time with her, Gabriel and the baby.

After that, I'm on my way to the Sunshine State, she thought happily as the van sped along the wintry Ohio roads. *This might well turn out to be the best month of my life.*

Jonathan Rocke tossed a shovelful of snow to the side of the driveway. He knew how important the snow was to his wheat crop. It provided insulation for the seeds now, and when the spring came, it would melt and provide moisture for the soil, as well. But today, he considered the snow quite literally to be a pain in the neck—*his* neck. His back and shoulders, too.

As soon as the thought crossed his mind, he felt guilty. He had no right to grumble, even to himself. It wasn't as if he were sick, like his brother, who had been lying in bed since yesterday afternoon. Or at least, Jonathan didn't have a fever like Gabriel did, nor was he coughing or in any pain other than the temporary burn in his upper-body muscles as he shoveled. He did, however, feel as if he were moving in slow motion. As if he were one of his own draft horses, pulling a plow behind him all day.

It wasn't just his body that seemed to be burdened with an invisible weight; his mind was sluggish, too. He'd concentrate with all his might and still end up forgetting half of the items he intended to purchase or chores he needed to complete. When he opened the Bible to read a passage of Scripture as he usually did in the morning, he couldn't retain what he was reading and he'd have to start over three or four times before it sank in. It was like this for him every winter, but this year was particularly bad.

Jonathan attributed his lethargy to not having enough manual labor to do outdoors, the way he did during planting and harvesting seasons. There was still plenty of labor that needed to be completed in order to prepare the farm for spring, such as maintaining and repairing the machinery, purchasing seed and fertilizer, figuring out and paying taxes, and attending farm shows and horse expos. But most of those tasks required less physical effort and less time outside than what he usually spent during the rest of the year.

But that couldn't really be the problem, because here Jonathan was now, outdoors and shoveling, but it wasn't helping him feel more energetic. On the contrary, it was making him wish he could go into hibernation. What he wouldn't give to go to sleep and wake up again when it was spring and the snow was gone.

That's not a gut *attitude*, he chastised himself as soon as the thought crossed his mind. *That would be a waste of the life* Gott *has given me. The life He gave me a second chance to appreciate.*

It had been almost eleven years since Jonathan was in an automobile accident that could have cost him his life. That could have cost *other* people their lives, too.

The car crash happened when he was twenty-five. At the time, he still hadn't committed to joining the Amish church and he'd been living away from his home as an *Englischer*, much to his father's disgust and his mother's dismay.

Jonathan certainly had a deep faith in Christ, and he loved the Amish lifestyle. But for Jonathan's father, farming was the only acceptable occupation for his sons. Jonathan would have much rather built houses than raise crops, like his father and his brother, Gabriel.

So from the time he was twenty-one until the time the accident occurred, Jonathan had rented a studio apartment in the next town over from Fawn Crossing and he'd worked with a small *Englisch* crew doing carpentry. He loved the work but he didn't love the *Englisch* lifestyle, and he never felt like he fit in. Because he hadn't been baptized into the church, he wasn't shunned by his family and Amish community, but he wasn't exactly welcomed by them, either.

When he was twenty-four, he met Lisa, an *Englisch* server at a local restaurant. She was so warm and fun-loving and Jonathan was so lonely he immediately fell for her. It was the first time he'd ever been in love and there was practically nothing he wouldn't have done for Lisa. So when she asked him to get an *Englisch* haircut, or purchase a cell phone, or get a driver's license so he wouldn't have to rely on his coworkers for rides to job sites, he didn't hesitate.

After a year of dating, Lisa told Jonathan it was time for them to either get married or break up and move on. Jonathan knew if he married an *Englischer*, there'd never be any going back to the Amish, but he couldn't imagine remaining in the *Englisch* world without Lisa. So he purchased the wedding ring she wanted and proposed to her in a fancy restaurant she liked. Of course she said yes and when their server realized they'd just gotten engaged, he brought a complimentary bottle of champagne to their table. Jonathan tried a sip, his first taste of alcohol, before setting it aside.

Then they headed to his parents' home—Lisa insisted on meeting them, saying it would likely be her only opportunity—to tell them they'd gotten engaged. Lisa had drunk a couple glasses of champagne, but she had claimed she was fine and having had such little experience with alcohol, Jonathan believed she was. Besides, he was concerned about what kind of tone he'd set for meeting with his parents if they saw him arrive behind the wheel of a car.

As they were traveling along a narrow, winding road, Lisa kept veering across the center line. But when Jonathan suggested he should drive after all, she had laughed and said, "You've been in the middle of the road for four years now. One more mile won't kill you."

It had just dawned on Jonathan that she'd been referring to his indecision about whether he should "go *Englisch*" permanently. He was about to make a retort when a minivan came around the bend. Either Lisa sideswiped the van or the van sideswiped her; it all happened so fast Jonathan could hardly remember any of it except the noise and the terrible jarring sensation before he and Lisa plummeted sideways off the low embankment, rolling twice before landing in an upright position, unharmed.

The other car wasn't so fortunate; it had slammed into a tree. As Lisa dialed 9-1-1, Jonathan climbed up the embankment. He could hear a child—children?—screaming even before he crossed the street, and right then he made a resolution: if everyone in the minivan survived, he'd go back to the farm and join the Amish for good. And he'd never, ever get romantically involved with another woman again, because he clearly couldn't trust his better judgment when he did.

Fortunately, the mother, father and their two daughters who had been traveling in the other car survived the accident with only minor injuries. Jonathan made good on his promise to himself to return to the Amish, a decision that seemed to infuriate more than sadden Lisa. Although it pained him to break up with her, he had learned she started dating another guy within two weeks and they got married some ten months later.

In the eleven years since the accident, Jonathan and Gabriel had lost both of their parents. First their mother, to cancer, and later their father died of a heart attack. And while Jonathan took less pleasure in farming than he did in carpentry, he consoled himself with the knowledge that his parents had been overjoyed by his return to the Amish faith and lifestyle.

They were especially relieved that Jonathan and his brother were working side by side on the family's wheat and oats farm once more. Gabriel had always been prone to illness, so Jonathan knew it was a comfort to his mother and father when he promised he'd never abandon Gabriel or the farm again.

Thank the Lord I never seem to lose my strength in the warmer months, Jonathan mused.

"It's almost lunchtime!" Jonathan's sister-in-law,

Esther, called to him from the porch, interrupting his thoughts.

"I'll be done in five minutes," he shouted back, and she waved her approval.

Jonathan was glad his brother had married such a wonderful woman as Esther. Not only did she partner tirelessly with her husband to run the farm, but she'd always treated Jonathan as if he were a member of the household, setting a place for him at every meal even though he could have fixed himself something to eat at his little house on the corner of the property.

Jonathan didn't have much of an appetite these days, despite all of the time he spent working outdoors, but he'd never turn down the opportunity to spend time around his niece. With her distinctly formed eyebrows, scraggly strawberry blond hair and infectious laugh, little Rebekah was the one person who always brought a smile to Jonathan's lips.

I may not have a dochder *or* suh *of my own, but my niece is the next best thing*, he thought as he stuck his shovel upright in the snowbank. Just then, a van rolled up the driveway.

That must be Leah, Esther's friend, he thought. He'd met Leah ten years ago at Esther and Gabriel's wedding, but that was only about a year after the accident and Jonathan had still been adjusting to living on the farm again. He couldn't remember a lot from that period in his life, other than that his mother had been dying and he'd regretted not having spent more time with her because he was living among the *Englisch*. His other memories paled in comparison.

"Hello. I'm Jonathan, Gabriel's brother," he greeted the trim, dark-haired, dark-eyed woman who got out of the van from the front passenger side. She was holding a large rectangular plastic container, and balanced on top of that was a cake box.

"*Jah*, I remember you from Esther and Gabriel's *hochzich*. I'm Leah," she said. The apples of her cheeks became even more pronounced when she smiled. There was something about her expression—the upturned nose? the lack of wrinkles?—that made her appear too young to be Esther's age. "As you can see, Esther's *mamm* loaded me down with her favorite treats from home—upside-down fudge cake and coconut macaroons. Would you mind helping me with my bags, please?"

Until then, Jonathan hadn't realized he'd been staring instead of moving. *"Jah."*

"You *would* mind?" She laughed, but Jonathan felt too doltish to see any humor in his response.

"*Neh*, I meant I'd help you with your bags."

He walked around to the back of the van and took the two suitcases from the driver. They were more cumbersome than he expected and as they walked up the driveway, he asked what she'd brought that was so heavy.

"Books, mostly, for when I go to Florida. I can't wait to sit in the sunshine and read to my heart's content, without anyone around to interrupt me."

Jonathan frowned, recalling how he used to read all the time when he moved away from his family. Until he met Lisa, books were his constant companion. He still enjoyed reading when his concentration allowed, but he preferred to pick up a book because he wanted to, not because he had nothing else to do or no one else to turn to for conversation.

"I can't imagine going all the way to Florida just to read." Jonathan was hardly aware he'd spoken until Leah replied.

"Well, then I guess it's a *gut* thing I'm the one going there and you're not." She said it with a smile, but he had the feeling she didn't mean it in a lighthearted way.

Leah couldn't help but notice the frown on Jonathan's face. Again. That's what she remembered about him most from the wedding, too—that he wore a vacant, sullen expression. Which was a shame, really, considering his face was otherwise pleasantly masculine, with its hawkish nose, sandy blond eyebrows and blue eyes that seemed extraordinarily large, no doubt magnified by the silver-framed glasses he wore. *He probably thinks it's self-indulgent of me to go to Florida, just like Catherine does. But the trip is a gift and it would be ungracious of me to act as if I'm not excited about going.*

After removing their boots and outerwear, they entered the farmhouse through the side mudroom door. Leah barely had time to set the goodies down before Esther came charging in to embrace her. Although Esther was born without her right forearm and hand, she gave some of the best hugs Leah ever received.

"You look *wunderbaar!*" she told Leah. "Even younger than the last time I went home to Bensonville five years ago. How is it possible you don't have any wrinkles?"

"Because I don't have a husband or *kinner* to give me any," Leah joked. "My niece and nephew have given me my first gray hairs, though. I think I've counted a dozen of them."

"Just wait until the grays start outnumbering the rest of your hair, the way mine do," Esther replied.

"You're so blonde, how can you tell? When I look at you, all I see is the young *maedel* who used to catch all the *buwe*'s eyes when we went on singings together."

Esther shook her head, as if to deny the compliment. She'd always seemed oblivious to her winsome appearance and she turned down one suitor after the next until she'd met Gabriel, who had come to Bensonville to visit distant relatives of his mother. Because Esther and Gabriel had had a long-distance courtship and then Esther moved to Fawn Crossing after the wedding, Leah hadn't gotten to know Gabriel very well, and she was looking forward to spending more time with him, as well as with Esther and Rebekah.

"Speaking of *buwe* whose attention you captured, where's Gabriel?" Leah asked as she, Esther and Jonathan stepped into the kitchen. "And where's that little bundle of joy you keep writing to me about?"

"Rebekah's napping and I'm afraid Gabriel is, too. He's been running a low-grade fever."

"Oh, dear. You should have told me, Esther. I wouldn't have imposed on you when your husband is sick." *And I wouldn't have risked getting ill, myself—I don't want to wind up with a cold on vacation.*

"I know. That's why I didn't tell you. I wouldn't have missed your visit for anything in the world. Besides, Gabriel's not that sick, he's just a little run-down. He's very excited to have you here, though."

Leah immediately felt guilty for worrying that she might catch Gabriel's illness and it would interfere with the fun she planned to have in Pinecraft. "I wouldn't have missed seeing you for anything in the world, either. And I hope Gabriel doesn't feel obligated to socialize—he ought to take as much rest as he needs. Besides, if he's in bed, that will give you and me more time to visit alone."

Jonathan cleared his throat. "I, uh, I'm not that *hungerich* if you two would rather eat by yourselves."

Leah hadn't meant to offend Jonathan; he was so quiet she'd actually forgotten he was in the room with them. She blithely pulled his arm, tugging him toward a seat at the table. "Don't be *lappich*, I didn't mean now! I meant this evening—Esther and I have been known to stay up until the wee hours chatting away. We can do our catching up then."

Esther chuckled. "I don't know how late I'll be able to stay up. Ever since Rebekah was born, I've been going to bed almost as soon as I put her down for the night. How can one small *bobbel* so thoroughly exhaust me?"

Leah knew Esther wasn't really complaining; everything about her joyful tone and facial expression indicated how thrilled she was to be a mother at last. But she did have dark circles beneath her eyes, so Leah offered, "If you need to take a nap after lunch, I'd be *hallich* to take care of Rebekah."

Jonathan cleared his throat. "Or I can watch her. I know you wanted to go to the grocery store this afternoon, Esther. It's pretty cold to take the *bobbel* out, so I could stay here with Rebekah and Gabriel. That way, you and Leah will have time alone to visit with each other."

Leah giggled at the notion of Jonathan babysitting, but Esther quickly told her he wasn't joking. "Right before *Grischtdaag*, Gabriel and I both came down with a twenty-four-hour bug and Jonathan single-handedly took care of Rebekah the entire time."

"Really?" Leah glanced at Jonathan, who looked as if he hadn't even shaved that morning and whose speech and actions were so languid it seemed as if *he* was the one who needed a nap. Or at least a strong cup of coffee. She couldn't imagine him interacting with a baby, except perhaps to lull her to sleep with his lackadaisical mannerisms.

"*Jah.* She's *narrish* about him. You should see her chubby little face light up whenever he enters the room, right, Jonathan?"

His ears turned red and instead of answering, he pushed his chair back and excused himself for a minute, saying he'd forgotten to wash his hands. Once he left, Leah scooped chili into three bowls while Esther cut a pan of corn bread into squares and buttered them. As they worked, they simultaneously discussed the latest gossip from Bensonville, as well as life on the farm in Fawn Crossing.

"Gabriel's *bruder* really has been a huge help with Rebekah," Esther repeated. "I don't know any other men—except for Gabriel, of course—who would help out with a *bobbel* the way he has. If he's this *gut* with his niece, imagine how he'd be with his own *kinner.*"

"I hope that's not a hint," Leah warned. "You know I have no interest in courting and even less interest in starting a *familye.*"

"It wasn't a hint—I was just commenting on how much I've appreciated Jonathan's help, that's all. Besides, he seems to have even less interest in courting than you do, if that's possible," Esther said. Then she added with a laugh, "Which I suppose means you two have something important in common so you'd probably make a really *gut* couple."

Leah had to laugh at Esther's twisted logic, too. "I'm relatively certain not wanting to court is the *only* thing Jonathan and I have in common. He's kind of… *schtill*, isn't he?" Although she used the *Pennsylfaanisch Deitsch* word for *quiet*, what Leah was implying was that he was *dull*.

"*Jah*, I suppose he is too *schtill* for a *bobblemoul* like you," Esther jested, fondly referring to Leah as a blabbermouth and making her crack up once again.

"I admit, I am more *babblich* than usual, but that's only because I'm so *hallich* to be visiting you before I go to Florida," she explained. "I can hardly contain my excitement!"

And if I didn't let Catherine squelch it, I'm not going to let a wet blanket like Jonathan detract from this blessing, either.

Jonathan stood in the hallway, waiting for Leah and Esther to change the subject so they wouldn't know he'd overheard them talking about him and think he'd been intentionally eavesdropping. They hadn't said anything that was untrue or unkind and yet he felt embarrassed by their remarks. But why? Although courting was a personal matter, Esther was right about him not wanting to be anyone's suitor, so that wasn't what made him feel chagrined. No, it was Leah's description of him that caught Jonathan off guard.

Schtill meant quiet, but it also meant still, or holding still. Which, considering Jonathan's general mood for the past three months, was the perfect word to describe him; inwardly, he felt as frozen as a dormant seed. He just hadn't realized it was so obvious even a stranger could recognize it at a glance.

But maybe Leah hadn't noticed his mood; maybe she'd only meant that he wasn't talking a lot. The way she said *schtill* sounded scornful to him, but Jonathan couldn't be sure; when he was this low, he sometimes interpreted remarks in ways they weren't intended. In any case, what did it matter what she thought of him? Today was Saturday and Leah was leaving early Tuesday morning. Likewise, his mood was transient, too.

"To everything there is a season," the Bible said. "A time to plant and a time to pluck up that which is planted."

Jonathan reminded himself that the daylight was lasting until a little after five o'clock now. Spring would come again and his outlook would brighten. Until then, he just had to keep going through the motions of his daily routine. *And at this moment, that means eating lunch with my sister-in-law and her* bobblemoul *friend*, he thought as he forced himself to rejoin them in the kitchen.

Chapter Two

Except for one trip to Lancaster for the funeral when Betty's husband died, this was the first time in almost twenty years that Leah hadn't slept in her own bed. So when she was awoken abruptly by Rebekah's cries the next morning, it took her a minute to figure out where she was.

She tossed back the quilt and slipped next door to the baby's room in order to pick her up before she woke her parents. Gabriel had only managed to come downstairs long enough to get a glass of water and say hello to Leah yesterday afternoon. And by eight o'clock, Esther looked so exhausted that Leah claimed to be too tired to stay up talking after all, just so her friend would go to bed early. If possible, Leah hoped they'd both sleep in.

As soon as she reached down and scooped Rebekah up, the baby stopped crying and looked at Leah with big eyes, as if to say, "Who are you?"

Leah couldn't help but laugh and the baby giggled, too. She changed her diaper and then brought her to the guest room and laid her in the middle of the bed. After getting dressed, Leah brushed her hair. She turned her back for one moment to glance in the mirror as she pinned on her prayer *kapp* and when she looked at Rebekah again, the baby was near the edge of the bed. Leah dashed around to the other side to stop her from falling off.

"Who taught you to roll like that?" she cooed, smiling down at her. "Have you been watching your *mamm* use her rolling pin? Are you your *daed*'s favorite little cinnamon roll?"

With each nonsensical question, Rebekah gave Leah a big giggle and then she raised her eyebrows and puckered her mouth until Leah asked her something else and then she'd break into a giggle again.

"You're the first person who thinks my jokes are *schpass*," Leah told her. "But we don't want to wake up your *eldre*, so let's go into the kitchen and get something to eat."

Esther had confided that she'd had to switch to formula when Rebekah was four months old due to insufficient milk supply, so Leah figured she'd prepare the baby's bottle. She sat her in her high chair and opened the cupboards to look for formula and infant cereal, but Rebekah immediately began banging on the tray.

"Shh-shh, you'll wake your *mamm* and *daed*," Leah whispered, a finger to her lips. For some reason, Rebekah found that funny, too, and she squealed loudly.

Leah scrambled to give her a couple of her plastic, doughnut-shaped stacking toys but Rebekah clapped them together twice and then threw them to the floor. As Leah bent to retrieve them from where they'd rolled under the table, she commented, "No wonder your *mamm* is so worn out. We haven't even been awake for ten minutes and I already want to go back to bed."

"You want me to watch her for you?" Jonathan asked from the threshold of the mudroom, startling Leah. As she straightened into a standing position, she knocked the back of her head on the table.

"Ouch!" she exclaimed vehemently. Maybe it was because of the fierceness in Leah's voice, but the baby screwed her face into a knot and began to wail. Leah had clunked her head so hard she felt like wailing, too.

Jonathan strode across the room and lifted the baby from the high chair. He barely jostled her half a minute before she was smiling again. Leah, however, was not.

"What are you doing here so early in the morning? You frightened me." *And now I've got a* koppweh, Leah thought, gingerly touching the back of her skull.

"I'm sorry. I always *kumme* here to worship with Gabriel and Esther on off-Sundays," he explained, gently bouncing the baby up and down, while also shifting from foot to foot. "My *bruder* is always up early and Esther is usually making breakfast or has a pot of *kaffi* on."

"Well, I was trying to let them sleep in, but after all the ruckus, they're probably awake now," Leah retorted even though she didn't hear any stirring from the room overhead. She hoped Jonathan didn't expect *her* to have breakfast on the table anytime soon—Leah's focus was on making sure the baby was fed, which wasn't easy to do since she couldn't find what she needed.

"If you're tired, I'll take Rebekah," Jonathan offered again. "You can go back to bed for a while longer."

"Who says I'm tired?" Esther snapped, irritated that he seemed to want to take over. Did he think she was incapable of caring for the baby just because Rebekah had cried when Leah said "ouch"?

"*You* did," he answered. Before Leah could ask him what he was talking about, he explained, "I heard you telling the *bobbel* you wanted to go back to bed."

"That was just a figure of speech," she said. "Besides, you shouldn't be listening to other people's private conversations."

"Is it actually considered a conversation if one of the people can't talk yet?" Jonathan countered.

Ordinarily, this technicality would have cracked Leah up, but she was embarrassed he'd overheard her babbling to Rebekah and her head was really starting to throb. "Maybe not, but it's still considered *private*."

"In that case, I'm sorry for the intrusion, as well as for startling you and causing you to bump your head." Jonathan momentarily stopped bouncing to look at Leah. His eyes were an inky shade of blue and it looked as if he'd done a better job of shaving today, because the skin on his jaw and cheeks was smooth. Leah noticed his hair was freshly combed, too. *If only he'd wipe that scowl off his face, he might actually appear handsome*, she thought.

Rebekah squawked, indicating she wanted Jonathan to keep moving, so he complied. There was something about such a tall, lean and serious man coddling such a little tubby, smiling baby that made it impossible for Leah to stay annoyed. "It's okay. I suppose I'm a little frustrated because I can't find where Esther keeps the formula and I think Rebekah is really hungry."

"I'll show you." Jonathan pointed to a freestanding cabinet on the other end of the kitchen. "Esther needs to keep Rebekah's bottles and food supplies at an easy-to-reach level. She's often holding the baby and with only one hand, it would be too difficult for her to balance Rebekah in her right arm and reach overhead for what she needs at the same time."

Leah was aware that sometimes Esther struggled with simple tasks because she didn't have the convenient accommodations most people took for granted. Not this time, however; the cabinet appeared to have been custom-made to suit her needs. Not only was it the perfect height for Esther, but the shelves slid out, too, allowing easier access to their contents.

"Did Gabriel make this cabinet?"

"*Neh*. I did."

Leah vaguely remembered Esther mentioning Jonathan had been a carpenter with an *Englisch* crew before he was baptized into the Amish church. Touched that he'd obviously put a good amount of thought and effort into making Esther's domestic tasks a little easier, Leah complimented him on his handiwork. She removed a baby bowl, spoon and container of infant cereal from the shelves and then asked, "Do you still make furniture or do any carpentry work?"

His face clouded. *"Neh."*

"Why not? With craftsmanship like this, you could earn a fortune. And since it's winter, surely you have time to do it?"

"I—I've put carpentry behind me—except for helping build *heiser* and barns for the *leit* in our district." Jonathan set the baby back in her high chair and she instantly began to fuss. "If you have what you need now, I'll go out to the barn. Since Gabriel and Esther are both sleeping, I'll take care of milking the *kuh* and gathering the *oier*."

*I suppose Esther was right. He is quite helpful,
even with chores that are usually considered "wom-
en's work,"* Leah silently acknowledged. *But would it
kill him to crack a smile?*

She tried to pacify Rebekah while simultaneously
measuring out the cereal, but it was of little use. As
soon as Jonathan left the room, the baby began to cry
and she didn't stop until her mother came to see why
she was making such a racket. And then, of course,
she was all giggles, the little scamp.

Even after he'd milked the cow and collected the
eggs, Jonathan dawdled in the barn. Maybe Leah
wasn't used to dealing with a baby in the morning or
maybe she was reeling from whacking her head on the
table, but she seemed kind of grouchy and he wanted
to avoid talking to her alone again. Especially about
carpentry.

Granted, she'd brought up a valid point; there was
no reason Jonathan couldn't work on an occasional carpentry or furniture project during the winter months.
No reason timewise, anyway. But what Jonathan didn't
want to tell Leah or anyone else was that he couldn't
get motivated enough to start working on something
like that, as much as he might have enjoyed it. He'd
never considered himself a lazy person before, but he
was starting to feel like one now. He didn't want to
call attention to it by telling Leah it was taking all of
his energy just to keep up with the winter responsibilities on the farm.

When Jonathan finally did go inside again, he was
relieved to find Esther sitting at the table, across from
Leah, who was holding the baby on her lap.

"Guder mariye," he greeted his sister-in-law as Rebekah reached out her arms for him to hold her.

"Do you mind taking her?" Leah asked, handing the baby to him before he could answer. "Esther is feeling under the weather, so she doesn't want to get too close to the *bobbel* in case she's coming down with what Gabriel has, and I need to turn the bacon over."

"I never mind holding this sack of sugar, do I, Rebekah?" Jonathan said to his niece, who smiled at him and then promptly drooled on his wrist. While he was aware most people would say he was spoiling her, Jonathan continued holding Rebekah on his knee throughout the meal, jiggling his leg to keep her content. *It helps to know I can make someone else* hallich, *even if I can't seem to make myself feel better*, he thought.

"I can hardly keep my eyes open." Esther had only taken a couple bites of scrambled eggs before she pushed the plate aside. "I'm afraid I have to go lie down until we're ready to worship."

Leah jumped to her feet and felt her friend's forehead. "I knew it—you're burning up!" she announced. "I'll get you a glass of water and something for your fever."

The two women left the room and when Leah returned, she said, "I'm worried about her. That fever came on very quickly. Your *bruder* seems quite ill, too."

"Jah, I've heard the flu is especially virulent this season. Should we say a prayer for them?"

The two of them bowed their heads and asked the Lord to heal Esther and Gabriel quickly and to keep the rest of them from getting sick, too.

When they opened their eyes again, Leah said, "I

think I ought to stay here a couple extra days to help out."

Jonathan hesitated before replying. On one hand, he didn't know if he had it in him to make small talk with Leah for the rest of the weekend, much less for several additional days. On the other hand, he was concerned about taking care of Rebekah, as well as his brother and sister-in-law, on his own. While he'd managed for a day or two at Christmastime, Gabriel and Esther weren't nearly as ill then as they appeared to be now, Rebekah wasn't quite so active, and he'd still had a small reserve of energy left.

"That's up to you to decide, either way. I—I ought to be able to take care of them." *With* Gott's *help*.

Leah bit her lip, seemingly as indecisive as Jonathan was. Didn't she want to hang out with him, either, or was it only that she hoped to get to Florida as soon as possible? "What if you get sick, too?"

Jonathan tugged on his ear; he hadn't really considered that. "Well, we just asked the Lord to protect us from illness."

"And I hope that's His will, but it's possible it's not," Leah replied. She was reflective for a moment before saying definitively, "I don't need a whole month to loll about in Florida. I can't leave on Tuesday morning knowing Esther's not well."

Leah explained she'd intended to take a bus to Lancaster County, where she'd join her cousin, Betty, and about twenty other people who were headed to Florida in a chartered minibus. Since she'd arranged to call Betty at two o'clock that afternoon anyway, Leah said she'd let her know about the change in plans and she'd reschedule her itinerary with the van driver and bus companies, too.

Once they'd finished their meal, Leah did the dishes while Jonathan took Rebekah into the living room and set her down to play on a quilt on the floor. She wasn't crawling yet, but she could almost lift herself onto her hands and knees, so it wouldn't be long before she was mobile. *Hopefully by then, I'll feel more active, too*, he thought.

While keeping a watchful eye on her, Jonathan skimmed the Bible for a passage the adults could read aloud together as part of their morning worship. But as it turned out, neither Esther nor Gabriel felt up to reading, nor could they sing. So they sat on the opposite end of the room and listened to Jonathan and Leah. After Jonathan ended their worship time with a prayer, Leah informed her friend she intended to stay a couple more days until they were well.

"But you'll miss your vacation," Esther protested. "I can't let you do that."

"I'll only miss a few days, and I'd rather stay here longer, anyway. I've hardly had a chance to get to know Rebekah—her *onkel* keeps monopolizing her!"

"I didn't mean to—" Jonathan began to say, but Leah shot him a look and shook her head. He realized she was probably just saying that about him because she wanted to convince Esther she had another good reason for extending her time in Fawn Crossing.

"But we didn't even go to the market yesterday. My cupboards are almost bare. What will you eat? What will you do for *schpass*?" Esther fretted as Leah took her by the arm to help her back upstairs. Meanwhile, Gabriel wobbled toward the bathroom.

"Don't be *lappich*. I don't want you or Gabriel to think about anything other than getting as much rest as you can. Jonathan, Rebekah and I will manage just fine. We'll be like three peas in a pod, won't we, Jonathan?" Leah asked over her shoulder.

"Absolutely," he agreed, hoping he sounded a lot more confident than he felt.

While Gabriel was still downstairs, Leah arranged Esther's pillows and quilt for her.

"I know it's a sacrifice for you, but it's a huge relief for me that you'll be taking care of Rebekah," Esther admitted. She eased herself into bed. "So I hate to ask this of you…"

"Ask me anything," Leah said. "I'm here to help."

"Would you mind if Jonathan joined you for meals? He's lost a lot of weight since Thanksgiving and he seems so down. Gabriel and I are worried about him."

I meant I'm here to help you, *not your grumpy brother-in-law*, Leah thought. But she replied, "Sure. I'll have him fattened up in no time." *But I can't make any promises about curing his gloomy disposition.*

After Gabriel came in with a hot-water bottle for his wife, Leah went back downstairs and announced she was going to make cheese-and-homemade-bologna sandwiches, a typical Sabbath lunch.

Jonathan thanked her but declined, saying, "You don't have to cook for me while you're here."

"I'm not cooking. I'm making sandwiches," she pointed out. "Besides, Esther told me you always eat here. You probably don't even have a box of crackers at your house."

Jonathan's ears turned pink. "She's right, but I can

buy some groceries tomorrow, so you won't have to think about making meals for me. You've already got your hands full taking care of my *bruder*, sister-in-law and niece. You don't need to take care of me, too."

"What kind of groceries will you buy? *Supp* from a can?" Leah scoffed. No Amish man she'd ever met could make much more than toast, eggs or canned food.

"*Neh*, I got used to preparing my own meals when I lived among the *Englisch*."

"In that case, maybe *you* should cook for *me*," Leah suggested.

"Uh, okay. What would you like to have?"

He is so *serious!* "I was only kidding."

"I wasn't. I'm *hallich* to help with whatever you need me to do. I can watch Rebekah or go to the market or cook."

"I appreciate that." She did, too—her brother wasn't nearly as helpful as Jonathan was being, at least not with household chores and certainly not with childcare. "If you'd continue to take care of the livestock, that would be *wunderbaar*."

Jonathan nodded, saying, "Of course I will. It's also important to keep the *haus* warm when Gabriel and Esther are feverish, so I'll *kumme* in throughout the night to replenish the wood and keep the fire stoked."

"*Denki* for the warning. If you startled me in the middle of the night the way you did this morning, I might come after you with a rolling pin. Then *you'd* be the one to wind up with an egg on your skull, not me."

To Leah's surprise, Jonathan actually smiled. *Maybe he can take a joke after all*, she thought as she smiled back at him.

* * *

Jonathan didn't really feel like eating lunch, but since Leah had insisted on making a sandwich for him, he forced himself to finish the whole thing. He figured it was equally futile to refuse when she offered him a piece of the fudge cake Esther's mother sent, too, so he accepted the generous helping she served him. It was a wise decision; lately, everything had tasted so bland to him, but this dessert was delicious and he polished it off in six or seven bites.

While Leah put Rebekah down for a nap, Jonathan went to hitch the horse and buggy so Leah could ride to the phone shanty. It was only a little over two miles away, but the windchill factor made it seem much colder than twenty-eight degrees and he didn't think she should walk. Besides, when the two women had gone upstairs together after worship, Gabriel had taken Jonathan aside and asked him if he could be especially hospitable to Leah.

"She's supposed to be our special guest and I know Esther feels *baremlich* that Leah has to take care of us instead of the other way around," Gabriel explained.

Jonathan thought it was ridiculous for Esther to feel that way; it wasn't as if they'd planned on getting sick. Gabriel's request made him wonder if Leah was used to being waited on. But Jonathan recognized that Esther and Gabriel had done so much for him over the years, and the least he could do was make an extra effort for their friend.

So when he came inside to tell Leah the buggy was ready and waiting, he added, "When you return, there's no need to stable the *gaul*. I'll take care of him."

"Really?" Her big brown eyes widened and she

tipped her head to the side as if she couldn't believe she'd heard correctly. "I'm used to doing that myself. You've already ventured out into the cold once. Why would you *kumme* out a second time if you don't have to?"

Jonathan shrugged. "He's temperamental. I don't want you to have to put up with his whinnying."

"Uh-oh. Speaking of whinnying, I think I hear Rebekah." Leah cocked an ear toward the ceiling and pressed her hand on Jonathan's forearm to silence him. They both stood there listening.

After a moment, he said, "I don't hear anything but I'll check. You go ahead to the phone shanty. Your *gschwischderkind* is waiting for your call."

"Okay," Leah said and gave his forearm a friendly squeeze before letting go. "*Denki* for being so helpful, Jonathan."

Maybe it was the warmth of her touch or the way she said his name or the sincerity of her gratitude, but Jonathan felt as if something within him was beginning to thaw. And as he dashed upstairs to check on Rebekah, for the first time all winter his legs felt agile and his feet felt light.

On the way to the phone shanty, Leah dithered over how long to delay her departure. She knew the chartered minibuses routinely took two days to get to Florida; they'd stop about halfway there and the driver and passengers would spend the night in a hotel just over the South Carolina border. The exception was if they began their trip on a Saturday, in which case, they'd spend two nights at the hotel, as most Amish people considered it inappropriate to hire a driver to transport them on the Sabbath.

I guess that means the latest I can leave Fawn Crossing and still arrive in Florida this week is Friday, Leah realized. *I'm sure Esther and Gabriel will feel a lot better by then.*

Leah figured rescheduling her trip with the same transportation company wouldn't be a problem, especially since she wouldn't be meeting Betty in Pennsylvania now and could travel on one of the minibuses departing locally instead.

Unfortunately, she soon learned the only seats available were on a minibus leaving the following Monday. That was longer than she'd planned to stay, but since she had no other option, Leah regretfully rebooked her ticket and then phoned Betty to tell her the disappointing news.

"I'm disappointed, too, but *Gott* is using you for His purpose," her cousin reminded her. "The ocean will still be there when you arrive next week."

"That's true," Leah agreed with a sigh.

Yet as she traveled back to the house, she still felt let down and she had to remind herself that three weeks of vacation was more than what many Amish people got in a lifetime. *At least I'll be able to do a lot of reading while the baby is napping*, she consoled herself.

But over the next few days, Leah barely seemed to have time to read the Bible for her morning devotions, much less to delve into one of the novels she'd brought from home. Either Rebekah was coming down with something, too, or she was out of sorts because she was separated from her mama, but she wouldn't nap for longer than fifteen minutes at a stretch.

Furthermore, the baby wailed so much in the evenings, Leah usually gave in and brought Rebekah into bed with *her*, which meant instead of reading, Leah had to turn the light off early. It also meant she usually didn't get a decent night's rest. Not that she would have slept well anyway, as she frequently rose to tend to Gabriel's and Esther's needs throughout the night. But when she did lie down again, she was too conscious of Rebekah's presence beside her to completely relax.

For the brief periods during the day when Rebekah actually did take a nap, Leah would use the opportunity to dash outside and hang laundry on the line. Gabriel and Esther were alternatingly experiencing chills and the sweats, so Leah sometimes changed their sheets three times in a single day. *So much for not tromping across the snow to get to the clothesline*, she thought wryly.

Between running up and down the stairs to look after Gabriel and Esther, minding the baby and keeping up with the housework, especially keeping all the doorknobs and bathroom surfaces sanitized, it seemed the last thing Leah would have wanted to do would be to cook for Jonathan. But because he took care of all the grocery shopping and errands, and he'd amuse Rebekah or set the table while Leah was preparing their food, mealtimes were a breeze compared to the rest of her day and she found herself looking forward to their time together.

"*Denki, Gott*, for this food and for giving us endurance. Please heal Gabriel and Esther quickly. Amen," she prayed when they sat down to lunch on Thursday.

Maybe it was because she'd thanked the Lord for endurance or asked for a speedy recovery for her friends, but when Leah finished praying, Jonathan remarked, "This sure isn't the vacation you bargained for, is it?"

"*Neh*, not exactly," Leah answered truthfully as she heaped ham and pea casserole onto a plate and handed it to him. As usual, Rebekah was sitting on Jonathan's lap and he kept having to elongate his neck or hold her hand down so she wouldn't grab his glasses. Leah didn't know where he got his patience; she would have either removed her glasses or set the baby in her high chair by now. Then she added half-facetiously, "But it could be worse—I could be sick."

"What were you looking forward to doing most when you got to Florida, besides reading?"

"Going to the beach," Leah answered without a moment's hesitation. "And going bike riding and learning to play shuffleboard. But mostly I was looking forward to not being responsible for anyone other than myself for a while. To just getting away and being alone."

As soon as she saw Jonathan's crumpled expression, Leah regretted her words. "I—I didn't mean that like it sounded," she said.

"No need to apologize." Jonathan abruptly stood and tried to set Rebekah into her high chair, but she stiffened her back and legs, so he pushed her into Leah's arms instead. "And as I told you, there's no need for you to cook for me, either."

Then he grabbed his hat and coat from the mudroom and strode out of the house without even putting them on.

For the past four days, Jonathan had done his best to support Leah however he could. He'd gone grocery shopping and to the pharmacy—even returning to the store a second time because Leah had forgotten to add diapers to the list she gave him. He'd assumed all the care of the animals and he tried to be helpful in the kitchen and to take Rebekah off Leah's hands whenever he could, too. He'd even set his alarm clock so he'd wake every three hours to check on the woodstove so Leah could sleep through the night without getting up to stoke the fire. And he'd done all this while keeping up with his—and Gabriel's—winter responsibilities on the farm. But apparently, that wasn't enough: Leah still felt overworked. The only thing she was grateful for was that she wasn't sick.

Maybe I'm *not the one who's lazy—maybe* she *is,* he thought as he opened the door to his little house and began unlacing his boots. *She's self-centered, as well. "Getting away and being alone"—that's something the* Englisch *would say.*

But deep down, Jonathan knew laziness wasn't the issue; he could see Leah was working as hard as she could to tend to his brother and sister-in-law and the baby, without falling behind on the rest of the household chores. And the truth was, Jonathan had been happy to help her. But that was just it—for the first time in months, he'd felt a burst of motivation. For some reason, knowing he'd be helping Leah filled him with a sense of anticipation and for the past three mornings, he was actually eager to get out of bed and begin a new day. But instead of appreciating Jonathan's efforts, Leah just couldn't wait to be alone. Which in turn made him feel like a big sap for feeling so enthusiastic about being around *her.*

If she's so eager to get away from me, fine, I'll keep as much distance between the two of us as I can, he decided. And then, his oomph utterly drained, he went into his bedroom, pulled the shades down and burrowed beneath his quilts for a long afternoon nap. It was as close to hibernating as he could get, and he didn't know why he hadn't thought of doing it a long time ago.

Chapter Three

After Jonathan stormed out of the house, Leah felt like crying, but Rebekah beat her to it. And as the baby cried, she kicked her feet out and sent Leah's plate of casserole skidding across the table and onto the floor. The dish didn't break but it clattered loudly, which made Leah flinch and Rebekah howl even louder.

"Shh-shh, sweetheart," Leah shushed her as she paced the floor. "I know you're upset. You miss your *mamm* and *daed* and now mean old Leah has chased away your *onkel*, too, hasn't she? But don't worry, he'll be back."

The baby sobbed even louder, as if in doubt. Leah kept jostling her the way she'd seen Jonathan do until finally Rebekah quieted, and a few minutes after that, she was asleep. Leah knew the child was overly tired, so she tiptoed upstairs and gingerly laid her in her crib.

She was creeping back down the hall when she heard Esther feebly calling her name. Leah entered the darkened room. Gabriel must have been in the bathroom because his side of the bed was empty and Esther was struggling to prop herself up on her elbows.

"What is it?" Leah asked. "Do you need help getting to the bathroom?"

"*Neh.* I thought I heard something crash downstairs. Is everything okay?"

"Everything is fine," Leah said. At least, it would be fine, once she explained herself to Jonathan. "Lie back down."

"I miss Rebekah so much," Esther moaned, sinking into her pillow. "I wish I could hold her but even if I'm not contagious any longer, I'd be afraid I'd drop her. I'm still so weak. Even the bones in my fingers ache."

Leah placed a palm to her forehead. "Mmm. You're still running a fever. If you and Gabriel don't improve by tomorrow, I think we might need to take you to the *dokder.*"

"We have a nurse practitioner—she cares for almost all the Amish in Fawn Crossing. She'll *kumme* to the *haus.*" Esther mumbled something else that was unintelligible but before Leah could get her to repeat herself, she was dozing again.

Seizing the opportunity while everyone was asleep to go talk to Jonathan, Leah scurried downstairs. She headed straight for the mudroom to don her coat and winter bonnet, but when she got to the kitchen, she spotted the overturned plate on the floor. Since she was hoping to persuade Jonathan to come back and eat lunch with her, she decided she'd better clean up the mess Rebekah had made before he got there.

She had barely wiped up the congealed mound of noodles and peas when she heard the familiar sound of the baby whimpering upstairs. *Oh well, maybe Jonathan will get* hungerich *and* kumme *back soon on his own.* While Leah regretted having misspoken at lunch, she had too much to do to waste any time worrying about a grown man's appetite—or his moodiness. *One more reason I'm* hallich *I never got married,* she thought.

But Jonathan didn't return to finish his lunch, nor did he show up for supper, which was actually just reheated casserole, since Rebekah hadn't permitted Leah to put her down for long enough to make a fresh meal. The baby was clingy during supper, too. After a few minutes of attempting to eat her meal with Rebekah on her knee, Leah gave up, not because it wasn't possible, but because it wasn't pleasant.

"Your *onkel* spoils you by holding you all the time, do you know that?"

"Buh-buh-buh," Rebekah answered, waving her spoon as if she were admonishing Leah for speaking poorly of Jonathan.

Leah glanced out the window. Jonathan had to feel famished by now; was he really so offended he wasn't going to come over at all? She couldn't let that happen; Esther would be upset if she found out there was a rift between the two of them.

"I guess we'll just have to go get him and drag him over here ourselves," she informed Rebekah.

Leah put her coat and hat on first and then bundled the baby up in several layers before trudging across the yard. It was only a little past five o'clock so it was still fairly light outside, and Rebekah was all eyes as she beheld the sky and snow and trees. It occurred to Leah she might sleep better—they *both* might sleep better—if they went for a short walk outside each day. *Maybe during a break from his chores around the farm, Jonathan will stay inside the* haus *in case Gabriel or Es-*

*ther needs something and Rebekah and I can circle the
yard a couple of times.*

She knocked on Jonathan's door with one hand and
balanced Rebekah in the other. There was no answer,
so she pounded harder, which Rebekah seemed to think
was a game and she made emphatic squeaking sounds.

When Jonathan opened the door, his hair was disheveled and he wasn't wearing his glasses, which
made him look less scholarly and more rugged. He
squinted at Rebekah, but addressed Leah. "I thought I
heard the *bobbel*. Is something wrong?"

"*Neh*. I've *kumme* to tell you I've got supper on the
table up at the *haus*. And I wanted to explain what—"

Shaking his head, Jonathan cut her off, "I'm not
hungerich. I don't want any supper."

Leah felt stung; wasn't he even going to give her
the opportunity to tell him what she'd meant earlier?
She shot back, "Well, *I* am *hungerich* and I *do* want
supper. But I can't manage to take more than two bites
because your niece wants someone to hold her at the
table. And since you're the one who formed that un-
fortunate habit with her, you can hold her while I eat."
She thrust the baby into Jonathan's arms. "Whether
you hold her here or at the *haus* is up to you."

She twirled around and started back across the yard,
her face burning both from the cold air and her hot temper. Before she'd made it halfway back to the house,
she heard Jonathan's footsteps crunching in the icy
snow behind her.

She stopped and turned. He wasn't wearing a coat
and his boots were unlaced; if he wasn't careful, he'd
slip. Since it was useless to try to take Rebekah from
his arms, she didn't offer. Instead, she slowed her pace

as she wordlessly led the way to the porch. Once inside, Jonathan unwrapped Rebekah's many layers while Leah poured milk and served them both casserole. This time, he didn't refuse.

After saying grace, she calmly told him she hadn't meant what she'd said about wanting to get away and be alone the way it came across. "I'm sorry if I offended you. I only meant that's why I *originally* wanted to go on vacation to Pinecraft. It has nothing to do with how I feel about being here or being around Esther, Gabriel, Rebekah and you."

"It's fine." Jonathan gave a half shrug as if it didn't really matter anymore. Or maybe as if he didn't quite believe her.

Leah was on the brink of tears. "I'm not as selfish as some people seem to think I am," she muttered.

"I never said you were selfish," Jonathan replied.

"That's not the same thing as not *thinking* I'm selfish." Leah poked at the casserole on her plate. The reheated egg noodles were gummy in the middle and hard around the edges, one more thing she'd messed up today. A tear slipped from her eye and she wiped it away with her napkin. She was utterly exhausted and at that moment, she felt like she'd sacrifice her trip to Florida if she could just go home where she could sleep without a *bobbel* in her bed.

Jonathan shifted Rebekah to his other knee and fed her a spoonful of pureed carrots, which she pushed out of her mouth with her tongue, dribbling them down her chin. Jonathan, whose blue eyes were focused on Leah, was oblivious.

"I don't *think* you're selfish, either. I've seen how tirelessly you've been nurturing Rebekah—and Esther and Gabriel, too. And I understand what you meant now. I shouldn't have reacted the way I did. I was just hurt because…because I was *hallich* to be helping you. I thought we made a *gut* team."

"Are you kidding me? We make a *terrific* team. If it weren't for you, I'd be completely overwhelmed, Jonathan. I've never had as much help with domestic chores or childcare from a man before. It's made me realize how much my *bruder* gets away with not doing with at home."

"Really?" He offered Rebekah more carrots but she grabbed the spoon, flinging orange mushy liquid everywhere.

"*Jah*, I can't recall him ever changing the *bobblins' windle*, much less setting the table, even when Catherine and I have both been ill," she said.

"*Neh*. I mean…" Jonathan was blushing. "I mean, do you really think we make a terrific team?"

"Jah." As she confirmed what she'd said earlier, Leah realized how intensely grateful she was for Jonathan. But there was more to it than that and she earnestly told him, "Not only do I need your help, but I enjoy your company. Eating meals with you is the best part of my day."

"It is?" Jonathan sounded surprised, which made Leah wonder if she'd been coming across as more cantankerous than she really felt.

"Absolutely. Although I'm not sure I can say the same thing for your little friend there," Leah jested, pointing to the baby. "I think she got more food in her hair than in her mouth with that last bite. It's in her eyebrow, too."

Jonathan chuckled heartily as he wiped off Rebekah's head with a napkin. "At least the carrots are a similar color. They almost blend in."

"Nice try, but *neh*. That child definitely is getting a bath tonight."

"I'll give her one."

"Oh, you don't need to do that. I wasn't hinting."

"I know you weren't. But you look tired," he said, studying her. Leah suddenly felt self-conscious that Jonathan must have noticed the dark circles beneath her eyes. Then he said one of the nicest things any man had ever said to her. "I'll clean up the dishes and put the *bobbel* to bed after her bath. You should go read for a while."

Leah was so taken aback she was momentarily speechless. "I—I can't let you do that. Besides, Gabriel and Esther need to be looked after. I was going to talk to you about them. I think we should ask their nurse practitioner to pay a visit if they still have fevers tomorrow."

"I agree. But that's tomorrow. For this evening, I can refill their hot-water bottles or bring them tea or do whatever else they need. Go upstairs and read— close the door so none of us disturbs you."

The suggestion was appealing but Leah couldn't let Jonathan do *every*thing by himself. "How will you manage to clean up the kitchen while you're watching Rebekah?"

"I'll manage the same way you or Esther or any other woman manages. Just because I'm a man doesn't mean I can't tackle dish duty. As I told you, I got accustomed to doing all sorts of chores for myself when I lived alone. Now, go ahead upstairs. I'll get the fire going extra hot and you can turn the lamp up and pretend you're lounging on the beach in Florida."

Leah giggled. "*Denki*, Jonathan. I'll be down in forty-five minutes. An hour, tops."

"Don't get sunburned," he quipped.

That really made her laugh. Or maybe she was just giddy from the luxury of leaving the kitchen before the dishes were done. She rose, went to the doorway, and then impulsively spun around and returned to give the baby a kiss on her sticky head.

"Behave yourself for your *onkel*," she said. Rebekah bucked upward and Leah quickly moved out of the way so she wouldn't get clipped beneath her chin. As she straightened her posture, her cheek grazed Jonathan's. She was so mortified she couldn't look him in the eye as she apologized, but he just coughed and waved his hand like it was no big deal.

Feeling utterly sheepish, she retreated upstairs as quickly as she could. She looked in on Esther and Gabriel, who were both sleeping soundly. Despite Jonathan's suggestion, Leah left her door open so she could hear them call if they needed her. Then she chose a book from the pile she'd brought and reclined on her bed.

Instead of opening it, she lay there with one hand on her cheek. *Thirty-four years old and I'm all aflutter because my face accidentally brushed against a man's face*, she thought. But it wasn't merely the physical contact with Jonathan that made her insides ripple like the surface of a pond in a breeze; it was how thoughtful he was being toward her. She knew she ought to dismiss this feeling that she was floating on air, but instead, she found herself savoring it.

Some twenty minutes later, when she heard Jonathan creeping up the staircase and then quietly singing to Rebekah as he filled the tub, she was still touching her face and her book was still lying closed at her side.

It's too late now, but I wish I'd had someone like Jonathan to help me with the kinner *after* mamm *and* daed *died...* she thought, right before dropping off to sleep.

After Jonathan gave Rebekah a bath, he tiptoed down the hall to her bedroom to rock her to sleep. He noticed Leah's door was open and he wanted to allow her to continue reading uninterrupted, at least until the baby was in bed. Maybe by then, he'd be able to wipe the dopey grin off his face. *Only a week ago I felt like I'd never smile again and now I can't stop*, he mused.

Undoubtedly, he was smiling in part because Leah's smooth, silky skin had brushed against his face, setting his senses on fire. But that was an accident and it was a fleeting sensation; what really made him euphoric was what she'd said about how eating meals with him was the best part of her day. *It seems as if she likes having me around as much as I like having her here*, Jonathan marveled to himself.

Then it occurred to him that if Esther and Gabriel were still sick, Leah could stay in Fawn Crossing longer. He immediately felt remorseful for having such a thought and silently prayed the Lord would heal his brother and sister-in-law quickly.

"Ah-ah-ah," Rebekah murmured. Her eyelids fell shut when Jonathan rocked backward and they sprang open again when he rocked forward, so he kept up the rhythmic motion until her eyes stayed closed the entire time.

Leah's right—I have to break the habit of constantly holding the bobbel, he thought as he continued to rock Rebekah a little longer, to be sure she was fast asleep. Then he very warily inched toward her crib and lowered her into it before slinking into the hall. He didn't hear any noise coming from Leah's room and he figured she was engrossed in her book, so he went downstairs to stoke the fire.

While Jonathan would have enjoyed chatting with her alone, he wanted Leah to have as much time to herself as she needed. Settling into an armchair, he spent the next hour reading the Bible and praying. Then his sweet tooth got the best of him and he got up to see if there was any more fudge cake left, but he was halfway to the kitchen when he heard Rebekah whining upstairs. He paused, listening for Leah's footsteps, but when the baby increased her volume, he took the stairs by twos and swept her from her crib.

After changing her diaper, he tried to rock her back to sleep but she babbled so loudly he decided to take her downstairs. He hesitated at Leah's doorway. He didn't want to wake his brother and sister-in-law by talking in the hall, nor did he want to intrude on Leah's privacy by poking his head in the door unannounced.

"Leah," he whispered. Then he whispered it again, and again a third time, but there was still no response. When Jonathan glanced in, he realized why: fully clothed, Leah was sleeping soundly with one hand touching her cheek and the other clutching a book at her side.

Jonathan cuddled Rebekah to his chest, warning, "Not a peep out of you."

He tiptoed into the room and turned off the lamp. He made it all the way to the top of the staircase when Rebekah gurgled. Jonathan flew down the stairs and into the kitchen before she started babbling at full volume.

"What's that?" he asked, holding her in front of him at eye level. "You say you want me to put you down? That's *gut* because my arms are getting very tired, even if you're wide-awake."

Jonathan took some measuring cups from a drawer and put them on the living room floor at various intervals. Then he set Rebekah on her belly, so the first cup was just beyond her reach, and he sat down beside her. While she was able to pull herself arm-over-arm across the floor, kicking her legs behind her, she didn't get up on her knees into a crawling position.

Remembering something Leah had said about the baby needing more exercise, Jonathan spread the measuring cups even farther apart. Each time Rebekah reached one, he'd urge her on by tapping the next one against the floor and she'd jabber gleefully as she set out again. Finally, she tired of the game, so he picked her up and snuggled into the armchair, hoping to pacify her into sleeping again.

He must have pacified himself, too, because the next thing he knew, he woke with his fingers interlaced over her belly as she dozed, faceup, on *his* belly. A quick glance at the clock on the shelf indicated it was two thirty. Jonathan's legs were stretched out in front of him and his muscles were stiff, so he had to slowly shift into a standing position.

After carrying Rebekah to her crib, he listened for

sounds that anyone else was awake, but he didn't hear a thing. Downstairs, as he added more wood to the stove, he realized the fire at his own home would have died out hours ago, so he figured he might as well sleep on Esther and Gabriel's sofa for the rest of the night.

Jonathan woke at daybreak, rebuilt the fire and went out to the barn to tend to the animals. When he returned, the house was still quiet, so he put on a pot of coffee. He was shredding cheese for an omelet when he heard footsteps overhead. By the time Leah came downstairs, he had set the table and flipped the omelet. It was almost ready to serve.

"Guder mariye," Leah greeted him when she walked into the kitchen with Rebekah on her hip. "Did you really put the *bobbel* to bed last night and now you're making breakfast, or am I dreaming?"

"You're not dreaming," Jonathan answered. He saw no point in mentioning the baby had spent half the night sleeping in his arms. "Have a seat."

Leah slid a chair out from the table, but instead of sitting, she swayed in place with the baby. As she moved, he caught the faint scent of lavender wafting toward him. "I'm so sorry I fell asleep last night. You could have woken me—but I have to admit, I'm *hallich* you didn't. I got such a *gut* night's rest and I feel a hundred times better this morning."

"You look better, too," Jonathan said. *Ach! What a clod I am.* "I—I mean you look like you *feel* better. More rested. Not that you didn't look *gut* before, but—"

"But I had dark circles beneath my eyes, right?" Leah cracked up, an indication she wasn't truly insulted, and Rebekah chortled, too. Leah gave her a little bounce, lightheartedly scolding, "That's nothing to laugh about. *You're* the reason I haven't been getting enough sleep."

After Leah told Jonathan she'd been taking Rebekah into bed with her at night rather than to risk having her crying wake Gabriel or Esther, Jonathan confessed he'd slept with the baby on the armchair last night for the same reason. Leah sympathized profusely, again repeating that Jonathan should have woken her up.

"You've really gone above and beyond," she told him. "I think you've spoiled me even more than you've spoiled Rebekah."

"Aha, I *knew* you thought I spoiled the *bobbel*," he ribbed her.

Now it was her turn to stutter. "*N-neh*, I didn't mean to criticize. I meant, you—you shower her with your attention."

Jonathan guffawed. "It's okay. You're right. I have been holding her too much. I don't want to develop a habit that's going to be difficult for Esther to keep up once she's better. So, starting today, Rebekah's going to sit in her high chair for meals."

He took the baby from Leah's arms and put her into her high chair. She went willingly, at first, and was content to stay there until Leah had finished feeding her her cereal. But after that, she kept reaching out her arms for Jonathan to pick her up and when he didn't, she clamored for his attention. First, by cooing and prattling, and then by scowling and whining. When her bottom lip came out and her eyelids formed into two upside-down crescents, Jonathan could hardly bear to look at her.

Fortunately, Leah loosened her from her high chair

and deposited her on Jonathan's lap. "Habits take a while to break. You've both done very well for today."

"She's got me wrapped around her little finger, doesn't she?" Jonathan asked with a sigh.

"I can't blame you—she's awfully *schnuck*," Leah answered. Then she put her hand to the side of her mouth, as if telling the baby a secret. "And I don't blame you, either, Rebekah—he's awfully kind."

Jonathan realized Leah was only joking around, but he felt his chest swell. An hour later, he was still reveling in her comment as he headed toward the phone shanty to call the nurse practitioner because neither Gabriel's nor Esther's health seemed to be improving. Once again, Jonathan couldn't completely suppress his hope that Leah might have to postpone her departure a couple more days.

His elevated mood made him recall how he'd felt when he first began courting—or *dating*, the *Englisch* called it—Lisa. It reminded him of the headiness he'd experienced in her presence and the way his self-esteem billowed when she paid him a compliment. And it made him think of how eager he'd been to get to know her and to hear her opinions and ideas.

Yet although his feelings might have been similar, the situations were entirely different. *I'm only showing Leah hospitality like my* bruder *asked me to*, he convinced himself. *If that makes me feel livelier than usual, where's the harm in that?* Because of his budding friendship with Leah, he'd been able to accomplish more in a single week than in all of the previous month, but it wasn't as if he was about to let his emotions get the best of him. There was certainly no danger that he'd do anything to compromise his better judgment, like cutting his hair or learning to drive, the way he'd done for Lisa.

And although I wouldn't wish continued illness on Gabriel and Esther for anything in the world, if they are still sick, who better to care for them than Leah and me? After all, as she'd said herself, they made a terrific team.

Since the nurse practitioner wasn't able to make house calls until she'd completed her last appointment at the clinic, she didn't arrive until after suppertime.

"The good news is, their lungs are clear, so I'm not concerned about pneumonia, which is also going around," she reported to Leah and Jonathan after she'd examined Esther and Gabriel. "The bad news is, they definitely have the flu. And while I do think the worst of it is behind them, it's difficult to say how long it will be before they've got their strength back."

She said that while she appreciated how committed the Amish were to honoring the Sabbath, she'd strongly urge Esther and Gabriel not to go to church on Sunday, even if they felt up to it. The nurse practitioner also informed Jonathan and Leah that the general guideline she gave her patients was not to go out in public until they were fever-free for twenty-four hours, because they might still be contagious. And since one of them could contract the virus a full day before showing symptoms, she advised that Leah and Gabriel wear paper masks to church, which she supplied.

"You're doing everything right, so keep it up," she encouraged them. "Aside from getting lots of rest and drinking plenty of fluids, all that Gabriel and Esther need at this point is more time to recover."

After Leah saw the nurse practitioner to the door, Jonathan plunked himself down at the table and released a heavy sigh. "I'm glad they're getting better, even if it will take a while before they're up to their usual speed. Please don't feel you have to stay here beyond Monday, Leah. Now that there's nothing serious to be concerned about, I'm sure I can take care of them."

Leah pulled her chin back, surprised. "On your own?"

"*Jah.* Well, not completely alone—Rebekah will help me," he joked, and the baby, who was sitting on his lap, echoed him with a grunt.

Leah felt completely deflated that Jonathan didn't seem to care if she left. For one thing, it indicated he didn't fully appreciate just how much work she'd done if he thought it would be a snap for him to do it all on his own. For another, she thought he *liked* having her there as much as he *needed* her support. But she wasn't going to plead with him to remain in Fawn Crossing if it didn't matter to him one way or the other.

Leah went over to the sink to finish drying the supper dishes, her back to Jonathan. "Okay, then, if you don't want me to stay, I won't."

"Are you kidding me?" Jonathan asked incredulously, exactly as she'd done the evening before when he'd misunderstood how much she valued his help. "I *do* want you to stay. But you heard what the nurse practitioner said. There's no telling how long it will be until Gabriel and Esther get their strength back. I don't want you to postpone your trip indefinitely."

"I won't postpone it indefinitely," she told him, turning to look him in the eye so she could read his reaction. "But I don't see any reason I couldn't stay another week."

"That would be *wunderbaar*!" The bright smile that lit Jonathan's face quickly dimmed. "Well, it would be *wunderbaar* for me, because I'd have your help. But you weren't expecting to work so hard when you planned your vacation. You should be having *schpass*."

Leah was struck with an idea. "I know what I could do for *schpass*. How about if you put Rebekah to bed and I'll make popcorn and we can play cribbage. Or checkers?"

"*Jah*, we can do that if you'd like, but I don't think it's going to be any *schpass* for you," he warned.

"Why not?"

Jonathan deadpanned, "Because I never, ever lose at checkers."

"Is that because you never, ever *play* checkers?" Leah gave him a saucy smirk.

"Ha ha." Jonathan rolled his eyes but she could tell he was enjoying their banter, too. On the way out of the kitchen, he very distinctly whispered to Rebekah, "Leah's going to be in for a big surprise when she finds out I always win at cards, too."

After he left, Leah reflected on how silly she'd been to think he wanted her to leave. Clearly he just hadn't wanted her to feel obligated to stay if she didn't want to. And to be honest, two days ago, she might have been tempted to take advantage of his offer to go before Gabriel and Esther's recovery had progressed further.

She never actually *would* have left early, of course; serving her friend's family in a time of need was much more important than vacationing. But now her perspective about lingering in Fawn Crossing had completely changed; instead of feeling tearful and at her wit's end, she felt cheerful and capable. *I suppose that's the difference a full night of sleep can make.*

Of course, the connection Leah was forming with Jonathan also made it a lot easier for her to forfeit seven days of vacation. While she was aware he probably would have been as considerate to any of Gabriel and Esther's friends or other relatives, she was utterly charmed that he'd made a point of giving her an evening to herself. In turn, she was delighted she could reciprocate by helping him for a while longer.

Besides, as it turned out, she couldn't imagine having a better time playing games with anyone in Florida than she had with Jonathan, even if he did end up winning at both checkers and cards, just like he said he would.

Chapter Four

❧

Jonathan and Leah had had so much fun on Friday they decided to play cards again on Saturday evening. This time, Jonathan enjoyed it even more because Leah baked a spice cake for the occasion and Rebekah had actually gone to sleep in her crib, so it was just the two of them, which made it easier to converse.

They talked about their childhoods and their families and what subjects they'd liked in school. Jonathan learned that Leah had wanted to be a teacher, but her plans changed after her parents died, and he confided how much he'd loved being a carpenter when he lived among the *Englisch*.

Jonathan hadn't had such a pleasant time since he was dating Lisa. No, it was even more pleasant than that, because as much as he'd enjoyed Lisa's company, it was always tinged with guilt because she wasn't Amish. The past two evenings had reminded him of an even earlier time, before he'd left to live among the *Englisch*. The exuberance he felt when he was around Leah took him back to when he was a teenager and he'd go to singings. Afterwards all the youth would play games and socialize and it seemed they had their entire lives in front of them. At that time, Jonathan still had hope he could talk his father into letting him become a carpenter.

I'm not a youth any longer and from now on, I'll always be a farmer, he reminded himself. But he *felt* young at heart. While he knew he couldn't let his feelings get out of hand, he couldn't deny them, either. Not to himself, anyway. And why should he? If the Lord had provided a warm, sunny day during an otherwise bleak, frigid winter, Jonathan would have thanked Him for it and made the most of how it boosted his spirits. Well, Leah's presence there was like a bright ray of sunshine breaking through the snow clouds, too.

So even though the pair had stayed up till eleven thirty the night before, Jonathan practically danced across the yard to his brother's house on Sunday morning. Leah was wearing a forest green dress that enhanced her smooth, creamy complexion and made her dark eyes appear even more striking.

"I just finished feeding Rebekah and I still need to get her dressed," she said as she tried to wipe in between the folds of the baby's neck with a washcloth. The baby kept arching her back and pushing Leah's hand away. "Would you mind asking if there's anything Esther or Gabriel need before we leave?"

"Sure thing." Jonathan bounded up the stairs and knocked on the door. Esther was in the bathroom, but Gabriel was sitting on a chair, sipping tea.

When Jonathan asked if he could bring him anything, Gabriel said, "*Denki,* but Leah's taken care of all our needs. She told us this morning she's not leaving till next week. Did you know that?"

"Jah." Although Leah had rearranged her itinerary on Saturday, she had put off telling Esther about the change in plans, for fear Esther would try to persuade her to go enjoy her vacation. "I made sure Leah knew I could handle things here myself, but she truly wants to stay."

"I can't say I'm not relieved. And Esther is, too. Although she feels *baremlich* that Leah is missing more time in Pinecraft, she doesn't want to overburden you with caring for us and the *bobbel* on your own," Gabriel said. Then he gave Jonathan a once-over and remarked, "Leah must be taking *gut* care of you, too, because you actually look better than you've looked all winter."

"Compared to you, anyone looks *gut*," Jonathan razzed him.

"I don't," Esther said from the doorway. Instead of wearing her usual bathrobe and slippers, she had changed into a dress and she'd clearly made an attempt to gather her hair into a bun, but Jonathan couldn't deny she looked unusually pale and frazzled.

As he assisted her to the chair by the window where she wanted to sit for a spell in the sunshine, he joked, "If you think you look bad, you should see your *dochder.* Leah fed her applesauce for breakfast and she got it everywhere, even up her nose."

"Rebekah's or Leah's?" Gabriel questioned facetiously, but Esther burst into tears.

"That's the first time Rebekah has tried applesauce and I didn't get to see how she liked it," she cried.

Jonathan looked out the window, trying to think of an encouraging response. He knew Leah had brought Rebekah to Gabriel and Esther's doorway a couple of times so they could at least get a glimpse of their daughter, but Leah said Rebekah had cried so hard when she couldn't go to her mother that Esther had gotten very upset, too. So now Leah only stopped in the doorway with Rebekah if the baby was sound asleep, but she never entered the room, for fear of Rebekah catching the flu.

Handing Esther a box of tissues, Jonathan said, "It won't be long until your arms are sore from lugging Rebekah around again."

"I know. And I'm so grateful we have you and Leah here to help us, so I have no right to complain. I'm just tired, that's all." Esther blew her nose before remarking, "Speaking of being tired, I would have thought you'd look bleary-eyed this morning. Leah told us how late you were up last night. From the sound of your laughter, you two were having a blast."

Jonathan knew his sister-in-law well enough to sense she was fishing for information about how he felt about her friend. Esther often tried to match him up, even though he'd made it crystal clear he had no interest in courting anyone. He didn't want his sister-in-law to think he had changed his mind just because he was enjoying Leah's company. He avoided her unspoken question, apologizing, "Sorry if we woke you."

"You didn't wake me. When I heard you in the background I actually thought I was dreaming until Leah told me this morning how frustrating it was she couldn't beat you at checkers."

"*Gut* strategy if you can keep it up, *bruder*," Gabriel needled him.

"What do you mean by that?" Esther asked her husband, who explained that as long as Jonathan kept winning, Leah would keep challenging him to a rematch, which meant he'd have a valid excuse to stick around the house after the chores were done and the baby was in bed.

"Is that true?" Esther pressed Jonathan.

"Of course it's true," Gabriel answered before Jonathan could deny it. "Why do you think he's been so chipper these past couple of mornings?"

"You'd better get some more sleep. Your fever is making you delirious," Jonathan heckled his brother. Yet as he shuffled toward the door, his face was aflame because Gabriel had hit the nail square on the head.

Leah had been looking forward to meeting new people when she went to Pinecraft, but instead, she got to have that experience by attending church with Jonathan. The church members were extraordinarily friendly and although she initially felt awkward wearing a mask, Leah noticed several others wearing them, too. Everyone Jonathan introduced her to expressed dismay when they heard Gabriel and Esther had been stricken with the flu.

"Ach! You must be itching to get to Florida," Nancy Ebersole, the deacon's wife, said after Leah explained how she happened to be in Holmes County for an extended period.

"*Neh*, there's still plenty of time for that," Leah replied as she rinsed a platter they'd used for serving lunch.

"Well, if they're not better by next *Muundaag*, my husband, Peter, and I can *kumme* and give Jonathan a hand. There are others who can help, too. Many of us have had the flu already. You needn't delay your trip any longer, dear," Nancy insisted. "A vacation like that is a rare opportunity."

"*Denki*, but I'm sure they'll be on the mend by then," Leah replied.

As much as she appreciated Nancy's support, Leah found herself wishing she hadn't mentioned her vacation in Florida. *If Esther and Gabriel are still sick, I want to be the one to help them—and Jonathan*, she thought.

But on Monday morning, neither Gabriel nor Esther had a fever, so by Tuesday afternoon, they were able to come downstairs and join the others for lunch without worrying they'd spread the flu. Their appetites still hadn't returned and they both felt haggard physically, but they were delighted to be able to embrace their daughter again. She, in turn, was over the moon at being held by them and she laughed and burbled and waved her arms with joy.

Leah sat back and watched. She was so thankful that Esther and Gabriel's health was improving and yet it felt almost crowded to have them at the table with her, Jonathan and the baby. She'd grown so accustomed to it being just the three of them. Jonathan was quieter than usual and she wondered if he was thinking the same thing or if there was something else on his mind.

By the time lunch was over, both Esther and Gabriel were bushed and they had to return to their room. Rebekah began to cry, which made Esther tear up, too. "If you or Jonathan can carry her upstairs for us, Leah, she can *kumme* nap in our bed."

Recognizing the baby was too wound up to sleep or to let her parents sleep yet, Leah suggested she should take Rebekah for a stroll outside first. "It's fairly warm and she needs the fresh air. Especially since I heard we're going to have foul weather for the next couple of days. I'll tire her out and then bring her upstairs to you."

Jonathan went outside, too, since he had to hitch the horse to go into town and purchase a part for a piece of farm equipment he was repairing. While he was in the barn, Leah stomped a path through the ice-encrusted snow in a big circle around the house, pointing out a squirrel and various birds to the baby, whose expression was full of wonder.

As she rounded the yard toward the stable, she slipped and almost landed on her backside but she righted her stance at the last moment.

Jonathan strode over and asked, "Do you think you ought to walk up and down the driveway instead?"

"There's not as much to see on that side of the *haus* and it's so close to the main road that the *Englisch* traffic startles the *bobbel*."

"*Jah*, but her *eldre* are watching us from their window," Jonathan said out of the corner of his mouth, as if he was afraid they could hear him. He reached to accept Rebekah when Leah held her out to him. "I wouldn't want them to worry about the *bobbel*'s safety."

Leah pretended to be indignant. "What about *my* safety?"

"You're absolutely right. Where are my manners?" Jonathan repositioned Rebekah so he could offer his arm to Leah, much to her chagrin. She hadn't been asking for help—she'd been pointing out that Esther and Gabriel might worry about her on the ice, too. Leah stole a furtive glance toward the window, where she glimpsed Esther, standing with her hand clasping the end of her other arm beneath her chin.

I'll never hear the end of this if I take his arm, she thought. But it would have been rude to refuse, so Leah allowed Jonathan to escort her to the porch, arm in arm.

Once inside, she took the baby upstairs. Fortunately, Gabriel had decided to take a bath instead of a nap, so Leah didn't have to be embarrassed in front of him when Esther hinted, "You and Jonathan looked awfully cozy holding hands out there. Does this mean you don't find him to be quite so *schtill* anymore?"

"I've gotten to know him better, *jah*," Leah allowed. "But we weren't holding hands. He was keeping me and your *dochder* safe, that's all."

"I might be sick but I'm not stupid," Esther taunted playfully. Leah was glad her humor was returning but she wished she wouldn't speak so loudly—Gabriel might hear her. "A man doesn't help a perfectly capable woman across the yard like that unless he's interested in her. You two are probably playing checkers again tonight, aren't you?"

"*Neh*, I don't think so."

It had, indeed, become a nightly ritual for Jonathan and Leah to play games and have dessert after the evening chores were done and the baby was in bed. But because of Esther's remark about Jonathan being interested in her, Leah feared she'd been giving him the wrong impression. She certainly valued his help and enjoyed his company, but she didn't want to encourage him if he thought they had any kind of romantic future together.

So that night she told Jonathan she wanted to go to bed early and he left shortly after supper. But once

Esther, Gabriel and Rebekah were tucked into their beds, instead of reading, as Leah claimed she wanted to do, she paced her room pondering Esther's comments. It occurred to her that she wasn't half as unnerved by the possibility that Jonathan had developed a crush on *her* as she was by the notion she'd developed a crush on *him*.

These feelings are temporary and so is this situation. Taking care of a bobbel *for a week is nothing like raising a* kind *until she becomes an adult. And that's the last thing I want to do at this point in my life! So I need to put any feelings of infatuation out of my heart entirely*, she warned herself.

The next morning, Leah got up and dressed herself and the baby, careful not to wake Esther and Gabriel. When she carried Rebekah downstairs, she found Jonathan was already in the kitchen. His nose and cheeks were so cold they stayed pink throughout breakfast. He explained that he'd been outside longer than usual, but he wouldn't tell Leah why. Instead, he suggested she and the baby should meet him out on the porch in a few minutes.

"I've got a surprise out there, so don't look out the window or you'll spoil it," he cautioned before leaving to get something.

"What is it? A snowman?" Leah guessed, but he wouldn't tell her so she followed his instructions. When she stepped out onto the porch, he was waiting at the bottom of the stairs with a wheelbarrow. It was piled with a soft bed of hay, which was topped with a folded quilt.

"What's that for?"

"Esther doesn't have a stroller suitable for the *bob-*

bel right now and I couldn't find the sled Gabriel and I used to use as *kinner*, so I improvised."

Jonathan pointed out the path he'd shoveled through the snow, down to the frozen ground. From what she could see, it appeared to loop all the way around the yard.

"You're *narrish*!" she exclaimed. Then she held Rebekah up as if to allow her to survey the yard. "Look what your *onkel* did for you."

"I did it for you, too," Jonathan said. "So you won't slip or tire out your arms holding the baby. I made a path to the clothesline, too, although you'd pretty much already worn a groove down to the grass."

"Denki." Leah securely propped Rebekah in the wheelbarrow. She looked like a princess on a throne and once Jonathan started pushing her, she made a contented "ahhh" sound, drawing out the vowel, her voice vibrating with the movement of the wheelbarrow over the hard, bumpy earth.

This man is worth his weight in gold. If I had a husband, I'd want him to be just like Jonathan, Leah caught herself thinking as she walked alongside him. He sure wasn't making it easy for her to stifle her feelings of attraction to him.

A few errant snowflakes drifted from the sky and landed on Rebekah's fleshy cheeks. Thinking the icy wetness would bother the baby, Leah was about to remove her own scarf so she could shield Rebekah's face with it, when Rebekah giggled and held her mittens to the sky, delighted.

As they passed beneath Esther and Gabriel's window, Esther tapped on the glass pane. Still dressed in her nightgown, she clapped and pointed to her daughter as Gabriel appeared behind Esther, watching over her shoulder. Leah could practically hear their laughter right through the glass window. The merriment was contagious and Jonathan insisted for the second lap, he give *both* Leah and Rebekah a ride around the yard. He tipped the wheelbarrow upward so Leah could gently position herself and the baby in it. They faced forward, so Leah's legs dangled over the side opposite from Jonathan, who worked his speed into a slow jog.

Feeling freer than she'd felt since she was a child, Leah sang the same "ah" sound the baby did, laughing at the way the pulsation tickled her throat as they bounced around the yard. By the time they'd circled completely around, the snow was falling steadily. Leah tried to convince Jonathan to come inside for hot cocoa, but he said he needed to return to town because the clerk had given him the wrong part. He wanted to get to town and back as soon as possible, in case the weather worsened.

When she went inside, Leah was surprised to find Gabriel in the kitchen, filling a pot to boil water for eggs.

"I can finish making those," she offered.

"Denki," he said, setting the pot in the sink and holding out his arms for the baby. "Let's trade."

"Do you think Esther will join you for breakfast?"

"Jah, she'll be down in a minute. She sure loved seeing Rebekah riding in the wheelbarrow. It was as amusing for us to watch as it was for the *bobbel* to experience."

"It was *schpass* for me, too. Jonathan came up with the idea and he cleared the path all by himself, because he saw what a hard time I was having navigating the terrain yesterday."

Gabriel gave a wry chuckle. "When I asked him to show you special hospitality, I never imagined he'd shovel the backyard!"

Leah's breath caught. Her chest hurt, as if she'd swallowed an icicle whole. So *that* was why Jonathan had been doing so many thoughtful things for her; his brother had requested it and Esther probably had, too. Leah should have known. They were still kind gestures, of course, but they weren't reflective of anything other than familial obligation and hospitality.

It serves me right to have the rug pulled from beneath my feet like that. Knowing I have no desire to get married, I never should have allowed myself to entertain feelings of attraction in the first place, she chastised herself.

Leah was relieved Jonathan was gone through lunchtime. She felt like he would have been able to see the humiliation written all over her face. At supper, she could hardly speak to him. Everything Jonathan said or did felt somehow deceptive, even though he probably intended to be helpful.

"Which do you want me to do tonight, put the *bobbel* in bed or clean up the kitchen?" he asked after they were finished eating. Esther and Gabriel were already in their room, since they'd had soup in the late afternoon and were too weary to keep going up and down the stairs.

"Neither. You've had a long day, between all that shoveling and running to town and back. I can do both," she told him.

"It's no problem," he insisted. "The quicker we get

done, the quicker we can play checkers. Maybe tonight is the night you finally win."

"*Neh*, I'm not up to it. I know when I've met my match and I concede you're the better player."

"Aw, you're not going to give up so easily, are you?" Jonathan jeered lightheartedly, but Leah wasn't going to fall for his antics. She didn't need him to entertain her; she'd have her share of recreation when she got to Pinecraft.

"I said I was tired," she snapped.

"Oh. Okay, then. I'll see you tomorrow." Jonathan was nonplussed by Leah's tone. Was it really that she was tired or was she upset with him? If she was, he couldn't imagine what he'd done wrong.

As he started toward the mudroom, Leah reminded him, "I need to go to the grocery store tomorrow and I'd like to go alone. But if Esther and Gabriel aren't feeling well enough to watch the *bobbel*, I'll take her with me."

Now it was painstakingly clear that Leah wanted to put distance between the two of them, so Jonathan didn't argue. "That's fine, as long as you're back by one o'clock. I have a meeting in town at one forty-five."

As he lumbered across the yard, Jonathan felt as if he had anvils for feet, and his heart was equally heavy. This was the second night Leah didn't want to hang out with him after supper. He would have understood if she just wanted time to herself, but he got the sense she was annoyed with him for another reason. Was it because he'd taken her arm yesterday? Or because he'd made a path for her in the snow? Maybe she thought he was crowding her or that he was coming on too strong.

I don't blame her. I've been acting like a fool—going out of my way for her again when all she really wants is to be alone. What is it going to take for that to sink in? he asked himself.

Jonathan flopped onto his bed, fully clothed. He knew it wasn't just his disenchantment with Leah that was enervating him; it was also that he'd had a disagreement with the vendor over the part he'd ordered, which cost twice as much as he'd expected to pay. Jonathan never liked the administrative aspect of the business—Gabriel was much better suited to it than he was and it depressed Jonathan that he'd made such a big error in estimation.

Added to that, it had been snowing—with more on the way—which made for precarious travel conditions and contributed to Jonathan's feelings of doom. As he was journeying home, he felt as if the gray clouds had seeped deep into his bones. Ironically, he'd been counting on Leah's smile to warm him. *Not even the* bobbel *was* hallich *to see me, now that her* eldre *are feeling better*, he lamented before dropping into an unshakable slumber.

The next morning there was an additional six inches of snow on the ground. Crossing the yard to the barn to care for the animals seemed as laborious to Jonathan as an Antarctic expedition. It took him twice as long as usual to finish his chores and when he was done, instead of shoveling the driveway, he went back to his own place to warm up first. He stoked the fire and then settled into the armchair and closed his eyes.

Indistinctly aware of the passing of time, Jonathan kept thinking he should get up but he must have fallen asleep because the next thing he knew he was woken by a persistent banging on the door. Leah was standing on his porch.

"Oh, sorry," he mumbled by way of greeting her. "You probably need to go shopping soon, don't you? Let me get my boots and I'll *kumme* out to clear the driveway."

"Are you joking? I've already shoveled the driveway and I just returned from the market."

Jonathan suspected *she* was the one who was playing a trick on *him*. "What time is it?"

"It's almost one o'clock. Do you want me to stable the *gaul* or are you going to leave right away?"

Dazed, he glanced over her shoulder and stuttered, "Th-the *gaul* and buggy are fine where they are. Do you need help carrying the groceries inside?"

"I put them in the *haus* already." Leah sounded annoyed as she scrambled down the porch stairs without saying goodbye.

Jonathan stood in the doorway, watching her go, a shiver racking his body. He knew he ought to hurry but he felt as if he was sleepwalking as he shaved and changed into clean clothes. He was halfway down the road when he realized he'd forgotten both his hat and the paperwork he needed for his appointment with the vendor, a fertilizer supplier. So he had to turn around and by the time he finally got to his meeting, he was almost forty minutes late. Knowing his tardiness reflected on himself and his brother, as well as on Amish people as a whole, Jonathan was overcome with shame.

When he returned home, it was all he could do to unhitch the horse, take care of the livestock and drag himself inside his little house. Even though it wasn't yet suppertime, he went straight to bed. *At least I won't have to deal with Leah's anger,* he thought.

But he was wrong; Leah came knocking on his door again. He'd barely opened it when she demanded to know, "What is *wrong* with you? Are you sick or are you just sulking?"

Jonathan blinked, hardly able to speak. "Sulking?"

"*Jah.* Because I don't want to play games with you in the evenings anymore."

"I was…I was giving you your space."

"Oh, so you're supposedly doing me *another* favor, is that it?"

He was completely befuddled. "What do you mean, *another* favor?"

"I mean that you've deigned to shower me with special attention by doing all sorts of nice things for me and making me feel like a special guest, but it's only been because your *bruder* asked you to," Leah clarified in a huff. "But now that I don't want to be the recipient of your…your *condescension*, you're sulking because you can't feel like you're Mr. *Wunderbaar* anymore."

"Mr. *Wunderbaar*?" Jonathan repeated incredulously. "I don't feel like Mr. *Wunderbaar.* If anything, I feel like I'm Mr. *Baremlich.* It's true, my *bruder* asked me to be extra hospitable toward you because he and Esther were too sick to treat you like the special guest you are. But that's not why I played games or shoveled a path around the yard for you, Leah. I did it because *I* wanted to. Because it was *schpass* for me and I thought you were enjoying yourself, too. I—"

His voice cracked with emotion and Jonathan cut his sentence short. He paused, took a deep breath, and started anew. "I'm very sorry you had to shovel the driveway this morning. I wasn't sulking. I was sleeping. But it won't happen again."

He started to close the door but Leah stuck her foot inside it and pushed her way into the kitchen.

"Sit down," she demanded, and he was too spent to refuse. She pulled off her gloves and put a hand to his forehead. "You don't seem to have a fever. Do you have a *koppweh*? You might be coming down with the flu."

Jonathan told her his brain felt fuzzy but he didn't have a headache. And while he had body aches, they weren't the feverish kind.

"It could be that you're on the brink of the flu, but the symptoms haven't fully manifested themselves yet," Leah suggested, frowning.

She looked so concerned Jonathan couldn't allow her to continue to believe his malaise was caused by a physical illness. "*Neh*, I'm not on the brink of the flu. The way I feel now is how I've felt all winter, except for a brief reprieve when...when you got here."

If Jonathan's earnestness and vulnerability hadn't already dissolved Leah's ire, his appearance would have. Beneath the overhead kitchen lamp, he looked more miserable than Gabriel or Esther looked at the height of their sickness, and she was overcome with sympathy.

"It's freezing in here," she said. "I'll make some tea while you stoke the fire."

Jonathan rubbed his forehead. "I have to go get some wood—I don't have any more inside."

He rose but Leah took him by his shoulders and turned him around, and then marched him into the living room and made him sit on the couch. "I've already got my coat on. I'll get the wood. You stay right here."

Once the woodstove was crackling again and they were both cupping mugs of tea to warm their hands, Leah asked Jonathan several questions about his mood and energy level. She listened as he confided how much he disliked wintertime and that most days, he struggled to perform even the most rudimentary tasks. He also told her every year he confessed his bad attitude to the Lord and asked Him to fill his heart with gratitude and his body with strength, but he still experienced a pervasive glumness throughout the season.

Finally, Leah gently suggested, "I do think you have an illness, Jonathan, but it's not the flu. I'm not positive, but I think you may be depressed, which could be related to something called seasonal affective disorder. The acronym is SAD, which seems appropriate, because that's how it makes people feel—among other things."

Jonathan shook his head. "That's not an illness. It's an excuse. An excuse *Englischers* use when they don't want to work. I *want* to work. I just can't seem to. Or if I can, it takes a lot longer than usual. It's a sin problem. A problem with my heart because I'm…I don't know, not appreciative enough for the blessings *Gott* has given me or something."

There were so many inaccuracies in what Jonathan had just said that Leah hardly knew which one to address first. "For one thing, SAD is, too, an illness and it's not just something that happens to *Englischers*. Our deacon in Bensonville was a very godly man—a very productive man, by anyone's standards—and he suffered from SAD for years and years. He tried herbal remedies, *Englisch* medication, getting more exercise, changing his diet, praying about it—you name it, he tried it. All of those things helped, but it wasn't until he moved to a little community in North Carolina that he felt like himself again and was able to function at his normal ability during the winter."

Jonathan set his mug down and pushed his hand through his hair, which appeared to be as close as he'd come to combing it all day. "I'm *hallich* that worked for your deacon, but even if I have SAD, I can't leave the farm and move to North Carolina. I promised my parents I'd never abandon it, or Gabriel, again."

"I'm not suggesting you need to do something that drastic. Like I said, I'm not even sure you have SAD. That's why I think it's important for you to consult with a *dokder*—"

"*Neh!* I could never tell an *Englisch dokder* how I feel, and I don't want anyone in my *familye* or community finding out, either," Jonathan protested. "So please don't tell them, Leah. The only reason I confided in you was because I didn't want you to think I was…I was being a jerk."

Leah remembered her deacon's wife sharing how difficult it was for her husband to seek help. She said he was afraid people might think his problem was that he was lazy, which the Amish considered a very shameful quality for a person to have. Leah knew she had to proceed cautiously if she was going to help Jonathan accept the possibility he was depressed and to do something about it.

"Okay, I won't tell anyone," she promised. "But I do have one stipulation. You have to agree to let me help you, as I see fit. And for now, that means you need to *kumme* up to the *haus* for supper and a game of checkers."

Jonathan's smile seemed forced. "That might make *me* feel better, but it's not going to help you because—"

"I know, I know. Because you never, ever lose at checkers," Leah said, her laughter belying how deeply concerned she was about him.

Chapter Five

Throughout the night, Leah kept waking and when she did, she vacillated about whether she ought to postpone her trip to Florida a little longer. Given Jonathan's current state, she was concerned about his ability to look after Gabriel and Esther on his own. Just as importantly, she was worried about his ability to look after *himself.* She figured if she could spend more time talking to him about it, eventually she might be able to convince him to see a doctor.

The only problem was that Leah knew Esther would object to her missing any more vacation time. Leah couldn't betray Jonathan's confidence, nor could she think of a plausible excuse for changing her plans yet again.

Dear Gott, she silently prayed. *If it's Your will that I stay here to help my friends, please show me how to make that happen.*

The Lord answered her prayers before noon the next day. It had snowed about four inches overnight and despite Jonathan's protests, Leah helped him shovel. She was waving goodbye to him as he headed into town when Nancy Ebersole came up the driveway.

"I imagine you've been running yourself ragged here." She handed Leah a round glass dish and a plastic container. "I thought I'd make supper for you tonight. This is shepherd's pie with molasses cookies for dessert."

"That's so thoughtful of you. *Denki*," Leah said. "Would you like to *kumme* in for tea? Gabriel and Esther aren't contagious any longer, although I don't think Esther will be able to join us. She's still pretty weak. She was upstairs resting when I came outside."

"I wish I could, but I need to go stock up on groceries before it starts snowing again. Did you know we're getting a blizzard on *Sunndaag* evening? A foot to a foot and a half of snow. Strong winds, too."

This news was so welcome to Leah she practically sang her response. "*Neh.* I hadn't heard. Since I'm scheduled to leave on *Muundaag*, I'd better rearrange my travel plans again."

"Ach! What a shame. Hopefully you don't have to delay your trip more than a day. Remember what I said. I'm *hallich* to help here. All my *kinner* are grown and gone, so my husband and I could stay overnight, if need be."

Leah thanked her, but when she went to the phone shanty that afternoon, she postponed her departure date until Monday, February 20—another full week—even though she could have gotten a seat on the minibus leaving on Wednesday, February 15.

When her cousin expressed disbelief that every minibus was full until February 20, Leah confessed she had an ulterior motive for remaining in Ohio that long. After telling her about Jonathan, she said, "I'm deeply grateful that you've invited me to stay in your bungalow, so I'm not taking that gift for granted. But I've noticed a marked decline in Jonathan's energy and mood since it's been snowing. I'm concerned the blizzard might drag him down further. There are people who could help care for Esther and her husband and *bobbel*, but Jonathan doesn't want anyone in his community to know he's struggling."

Betty clicked her tongue against her teeth in sympathy. "It sounds like he needs some sunshine. You ought to tell him to hop on a minibus to Florida with you."

Leah sighed. "I wish that were possible. But even if I could convince him to *kumme*, where would he stay?"

"Funny you should ask," Betty said with a chuckle. "I've met a Mennonite man, Moses Kasdorf, who came down here to work on *heiser* that were damaged by the hurricane last fall. He's shorthanded because two of his *suh* had to stay behind in Maryland with the flu. He's offering a place to stay and a small salary in exchange for construction work."

Silently thanking the Lord for providing for her specific needs before she even knew to pray about them, Leah jotted down the man's contact information. *A dose of sunshine and carpentry would be perfect for Jonathan*, she thought. And she couldn't deny that being around Jonathan in Florida seemed like it would be perfect for her, too.

Esther, however, was beside herself when she heard Leah was staying in Fawn Crossing another full week. Fortunately, she must have assumed there weren't any other seats available until the twentieth, so Leah didn't have to be forthcoming with the details.

"I'm *hallich* I get to have you here with me still, but this means you'll only have a week in Florida."

"That's still enough time to learn to play shuffleboard," Leah assured her friend.

Gabriel and Jonathan also took it for granted that Leah was staying until the following Monday because there were no seats available on any minibuses leaving earlier. She felt a little guilty for not disabusing them of that notion. If they had asked her directly, she would have told them she'd had the option of leaving earlier, but she was glad when they didn't.

Over the course of the next few days, Leah took every opportunity to spend time alone—primarily, while shoveling—with Jonathan. She knew if she was going to persuade him to join her in Florida, she'd first have to convince him he might be suffering from a lack of sunlight.

While the blizzard on Sunday night dumped a foot of snow on Holmes County, the sun came out by late Monday morning. Jonathan and Leah shoveled intermittently throughout the day and by three o'clock, the driveway was as dry as a bone.

"I can't help but notice you're more cheerful than usual this afternoon," Leah remarked as she stomped off her boots on the porch. "I wonder if that's because, despite the snowfall, the sun is shining brightly again."

"You're still trying to convince me I have SAD, aren't you?" Jonathan asked.

"*Neh*, not exactly." Leah hesitated. It would have been the perfect chance to tell him about the opportunity in Pinecraft, if only Jonathan weren't so eager to get inside and warm up. So Leah just said, "As I keep telling you, only a *dokder* is qualified to diagnose you.

But I definitely notice you smile more when the sun comes out."

"Maybe I'm smiling for a different reason," he teased.

"Like what?"

"That's for me to know and you to find out."

"Maybe *I* have a secret, too," Leah countered. And as she opened the mudroom door, she decided, *And tomorrow's the day I tell him what it is!*

When Jonathan woke on Tuesday, February 14, his first thoughts were of Leah. Actually, they were about what Leah kept suggesting about him having SAD. The story she'd shared about her deacon sure seemed to match what Jonathan had experienced himself and the more he thought about it, the more it seemed Leah might be right; he might need to see a doctor.

But today, he had other plans. Ever since he'd nearly broken down in front of Leah, she'd been especially tenderhearted and helpful to him and even though he was embarrassed by his own behavior, he wanted to show her how much he appreciated hers. And since the Lord had blessed him with Leah's presence for another week, Jonathan thought Valentine's Day was the perfect occasion to demonstrate a token of his…affection. Yes, it was definitely affection, as much as it was appreciation, that he felt for her.

After caring for the animals and milking the cow, Jonathan fetched the pint of white paint he'd been keeping at room temperature, along with a paintbrush, from his kitchen. He went back outside and, using a straightedge, he proceeded to paint the semblance of a shuffleboard design on the surface of the driveway. Although the pavement was cold so the paint wasn't adhering as well as it would have in the summer, in the end, Jonathan was pleased with the results.

Once he put the paint away, he went next door for breakfast. Surprisingly, Gabriel and Esther were already at the kitchen table, sipping coffee. On her hands and knees on the floor, Rebekah was rocking in place like a pony whose hooves were nailed to the ground. Adding to the festive mood, Leah announced she was making heart-shaped pancakes, topped with strawberries and cream and a drizzle of chocolate, as her little gift to everyone.

"So, what did *you* get me for Valentine's Day?" Esther teased Gabriel.

"Probably the same thing you got for me," he replied. "A germ-free kiss."

"That's the best gift I can think of," Esther answered with a giggle, bending over her knees toward Rebekah. She clapped her hand against her arm twice, saying, "*Kumme* to *mamm*, Rebekah. *Kumme* to *mamm*."

At her mother's beckoning, Rebekah abruptly starting crawling across the floor, hesitantly at first, but then gaining speed as everyone cheered her on. When she reached her mother, Esther swept her into her arms, laughing. "I take back what I said, Gabriel. Seeing Rebekah crawl for the first time was the best gift I could think of!"

Jonathan hoped Leah would feel the same way about her surprise, but since the paint was still drying, he waited until they'd both finished their morning chores before he invited her outside to see it. Leah looked curiously at him, but she put on her coat and bonnet and followed him onto the porch.

When he handed her a broom, her mouth drooped. "You brought me out here to sweep the porch? *That's* the surprise?"

"*Neh.* The broom isn't for sweeping." Jonathan hopped down the porch stairs, pointing to the driveway. "*Kumme* see."

The gleeful expression on Leah's face when she spotted the shuffleboard court and the round wooden discs he'd fashioned told him how much she liked them, even before she exclaimed, "This is the best Valentine's Day surprise I've ever received!"

She threw her arms out and for one split second— one *hopeful* second—Jonathan thought she was going to embrace him, but instead she twirled around with excitement.

"I didn't have time to make shuffleboard sticks, so we'll have to take turns using the broom as a cue," Jonathan explained. "But this will at least get you into practice before you go to Pinecraft."

"It can help *you* get into practice before *you* go to Pinecraft, too," Leah said, tilting her chin upward so she could look him in the eye. Then she proceeded to tell him about an opportunity to repair houses in Florida for a couple of weeks, possibly longer. She said the warm weather might be exactly what he needed and that Nancy Ebersole had repeatedly expressed her willingness to stay with Esther and Gabriel during their continued recovery.

As Leah studied Jonathan with those big, doe-like eyes of hers, he wanted nothing more than to accompany her to Florida. Yet he heard himself resisting. "I'd love to go. But what excuse would I give for running off on a vacation?"

"*I'm* running off on a vacation and I don't feel the need to justify it."

"I didn't mean that to sound like a criticism. I only mean…I'd feel guilty. I promised I'd never abandon the farm again. Gabriel would be disappointed in me."

"You aren't abandoning it—you're coming back in a few weeks. I realize you don't want Gabriel and Esther to know how out of sorts you've been feeling, but the truth is, they've already noticed it and they're worried about you. I think they'd be relieved you're doing something to take care of yourself."

Jonathan nodded slowly. "Okay. I'll talk to them about it."

"*Jah!*" Leah cheered, clapping her gloved hands together. "The sunshine will change your perspective and renew your strength. You'll see."

I don't know if the warmer weather will help me, Jonathan thought as he beheld Leah's smile. *But being with you will do me a world of good.*

As Leah suspected, Esther and Gabriel fully supported Jonathan's plan to go to Pinecraft with Leah. Also as she suspected, Esther teased Leah about it relentlessly.

"If you end up marrying Jonathan, will that make you my sister-in-law?"

"Who said anything about getting married?"

"The way you two look at each other says it all," Esther taunted. "Why are you so averse to getting married, anyway?"

Although Leah pretended not to hear her friend, she'd been asking herself the same question lately. She knew what her response would have been before she met Jonathan: Leah didn't want to have a baby and go through raising children again. But these past couple of weeks had caused her to realize how much easier it was to care for a child and a house when she had a man to help her. Particularly, a man like Jonathan.

If she wasn't mistaken, his feelings about courting may have changed, too. At least, she surmised as much, judging from his comments and gestures toward her. Maybe a change of scenery would boost his self-esteem— who knew, maybe he'd even feel confident enough to ask to become her long-distance suitor. *But right now, his health is the top priority*, she reminded herself.

Knowing how overwhelmed Jonathan was feeling and concerned he'd back out of the trip, Leah helped him prepare by ironing his summer shirts, contacting Moses Kasdorf on his behalf and booking a ticket for him. Blessedly, Jonathan got the last available seat on Monday's minibus—otherwise, he wouldn't have been able to leave until Thursday. Granted, Jonathan wasn't sitting next to her, but she figured someone would switch places with them once they boarded.

"Are you sure you have everything you need?" Esther asked her on Monday morning, shortly before the van driver was scheduled to pick up Leah and Jonathan and take them to the bus station.

Leah had just come downstairs from tucking Rebekah in for her midmorning nap and she took a seat beside her friend on the couch. Gabriel was resting, too, and Jonathan was taking care of some last-minute business at the bank in town.

"*Jah.* Unless you'll let me take the *bobbel* with us. I'm going to miss her terribly."

"Sorry, but Gabriel and I will be lonely enough

as it is without you and Jonathan here," Esther said. "Shouldn't he be back by now?"

Leah glanced at the clock. It was ten forty-five. The van driver would pick them up at eleven; the minibus departed from the station at noon.

"I'm sure he'll be here any minute," she said, even though she was beginning to wonder what was keeping him, too.

Jonathan felt like it was difficult to breathe, so he unwound the scarf from his neck. Traffic on the main road had come to a standstill. For what must have been half an hour, he had struggled to keep the horse from getting agitated. He'd struggled to keep *himself* from getting agitated, too. Because there were cars behind him and in front of him, and snowbanks on both sides, there was no way he could change direction. He was stuck.

Although he didn't wear a watch, Jonathan figured it must have been close to eleven o'clock and he was still at least twenty minutes from home. Knowing how devastated Leah would be if they missed the minibus, Jonathan prayed, *Please, Lord, let the traffic start moving again.*

When at least fifteen more minutes passed and Jonathan realized there was no way he'd get home in time to catch the minibus, he began to wonder, *What if this is* Gott*'s way of keeping me in Fawn Crossing?* He tried to banish the thought from his mind, but the longer he was delayed, the more it seemed a likely possibility.

Finally, the police officer waved Jonathan's lane forward and as his horse slowly clip-clopped down the road, Jonathan spied the cause of the delay: a green minivan had crashed into a telephone pole. Its front hood was crumpled, the windshield was smashed, and the engine and hood were a gnarl of metal. When he spied a child's car seat in the back of the vehicle, Jonathan had such a vivid recollection of the accident he'd been in with Lisa, his stomach lurched.

As soon as he could, he turned off the main thoroughfare and onto a side street. He got out of the buggy, pacing back and forth, his queasiness worsening as memories swirled in his mind; not just memories of the accident, but also of his mother's death and his father's disappointment. Even remembering the jubilant expressions on his parents' faces when he came home for good caused his stomach to cramp. The guilt was overpowering and he retched into the snowbank.

What was I thinking, to imagine I need a vacation? The same thing that happened with Lisa is happening with Leah—I've let her talk me into doing something she *wants me to do, when my responsibility should be to my* familye. *Am I really so lonely that I've lost all my common sense again?*

Jonathan climbed into the buggy and headed toward home, trying to think of how to tell Leah he wasn't going to Florida with her after all. He knew she'd be disappointed by his decision and she'd likely be furious he'd caused her to miss the bus, too. *Maybe there's a chance she left without me and I won't have to deal with her reaction in person*, Jonathan thought. But he doubted Leah would do something like that.

Sure enough, he hadn't even made it up the driveway before she came rushing out of the house, her coat and bonnet on. She must have been watching for him. He halted the horse and got out of the carriage.

Leah's nose was pink and her lips and eyes were swollen, as if she'd been crying. "Jonathan! I was so worried about you. What happened?"

"I'm so sorry, Leah," he apologized. "There was an accident in town. I couldn't get past it. I know the bus has left by now."

Adding to his deep disgrace, she flung her arms around him and said, "That doesn't matter I'm just glad you're okay. We can catch a regular *Englisch* bus tomorrow. It will cost more, but it's worth it."

Jonathan stiffened and pushed her arms away from him. As quickly and firmly as he could, he told her, "I've changed my mind. I'm not going to go to Florida, after all."

Leah took a step backward. "You—you're joking, right?"

"*Neh.* I couldn't be more serious." Jonathan couldn't stand to look at the devastated expression on Leah's face, so he stepped around her to lead the horse to the barn, but Leah dashed in front of him and blocked his way.

"Why? What made you change your mind?" she asked, her eyes welling.

"I've got responsibilities here."

"So does Moses Kasdorf. You gave him your word you'd go help him. He's counting on you."

Frustrated that Leah didn't seem to care as much about him as she cared about her cousin's acquaintance, he snapped, "And who's to blame for that?"

"What do you mean, *to blame*?"

"You're the one who arranged for me to work for him."

"But I thought you agreed it would be helpful if—"

"Stop badgering me!" Jonathan cut her off. "*You* were the one who thought it would be helpful for me to go to Florida. And I can understand why it would be *schpass* for you to have a traveling companion, but I can't be so self-indulgent as to take off for the beach just because the mood strikes me."

Furious at what Jonathan was implying, Leah thrust her chin in the air and spouted off, "There's nothing more self-indulgent than sitting around and wallowing in your own misery and making everyone else miserable, too. You can go crawl into a cave and waste the rest of the winter pouting for all I care, Jonathan Rocke, but if you didn't want to go to Florida, you should have had the decency to tell me before you ruined *my* travel plans!"

Leah was so livid she could hardly see straight as she stormed back to the house. When she got inside, she poured out her heart to Esther, who suggested Gabriel should go try to change Jonathan's mind.

"Neh!" Leah uttered, dabbing her tears with her sleeve. "That's the last thing I want!"

Esther offered to fix her a bowl of soup for lunch, but Leah was too upset to eat. Because the chartered minibuses that catered to the Amish were all full until Thursday, she wanted to purchase a ticket on a regular bus. And since the larger *Englisch* transportation company wouldn't reserve a ticket over the phone without a credit card, and the Amish didn't use credit cards, Leah knew she'd have to go to the station in person. But first, the horse needed time to rest and she needed time to compose herself, so she went upstairs to her room and closed the door.

Weeping into the pillow, she thought, *My first impression of Jonathan was that he was surly and judgmental, and I was right. How dare he imply I was being selfish when all I've ever done is put his needs and the needs of his* bruder's familye *first?*

As disgusted as she was with Jonathan, Leah was even more disgusted with herself for being so gullible. For believing that he was different and that he truly cared about her, when really he'd just been pretending to be supportive and helpful. Clearly, he couldn't keep up the act. She should have known better. *I'm just glad I didn't allow myself to get even more emotionally involved with him than I did*, she tried to tell herself, but it was a small consolation, considering how much her heart was already aching.

When Jonathan heard footsteps on his porch, he assumed it was Leah coming to try to convince him to go with her to Pinecraft. Or at least coming to apologize. Instead, it was Gabriel who rapped on the door and then let himself in without waiting for Jonathan to open it. His brother didn't mince any words, saying, "I think you made a big mistake by canceling your trip to Florida."

"Did Leah send you here to tell me that?"

No doubt tired from trekking across the yard, the farthest he'd walked in weeks, Gabriel dropped into a chair. "*Neh*, definitely not. I doubt she wants to be within ten miles of you and quite frankly, I wouldn't blame her. It wasn't right to give her your word and then change your mind, especially after all she did to arrange the trip."

"I gave *Mamm* and *Daed* my word I'd stay on the

farm and she knew that. It wasn't right of *her* to try to convince me to violate my conscience. She reminds me of Lisa."

"You were only going to be gone for a couple of weeks, Jonathan, and you would have been staying with Mennonites and other Amish people. That's not the same thing as when you went to live among the *Englisch* for four years." When Jonathan didn't respond, Gabriel shook his head and pushed against the table to rise into a standing position. "The only similarity between Leah and Lisa is their names. It's a pity you can't recognize that. And it's a pity you have the opportunity to live the abundant life God would want you to live, but you're rejecting it out of some false sense of guilt."

After his brother left, Jonathan leaned against the kitchen sink, rubbing his temples. He didn't care if his brother thought he was making a mistake; he wasn't changing his mind about going to Pinecraft. But he supposed he ought to make it up to Leah for missing her bus, even if it wasn't his fault he'd been delayed.

Waiting until the horse was well rested, Jonathan headed to town to purchase a ticket for a seat on a regular *Englisch* bus. Fortunately, there was one departing early the next morning and although there were a couple of transfers along the way, there weren't any layovers, which meant Leah would arrive in Pinecraft by Wednesday. She might be more tired, but essentially she'd get there at the same time as if she went on the minibus and stayed overnight in South Carolina.

On his way home, Jonathan stopped at the phone shanty to call Moses and tell him he wouldn't be joining his construction crew after all. When he picked up the phone, he heard the familiar rapid beeping that meant someone had left a message, so he dialed into the voice mail system.

"This is Betty Zehr. I'm calling for Leah Zehr, who is staying at Esther and Gabriel Rocke's home. If you could please ask her to call me, I'd appreciate it. *Denki*," Leah's cousin said, before leaving her phone number.

Knowing his horse shouldn't make another trip later that evening and it would be too dark for Leah to walk to the shanty by the time he relayed her cousin's message, Jonathan reluctantly dialed the number Betty had left. Apparently she was staying in an *Englisch*-owned rental in Florida, because she picked up right away. When Jonathan explained who he was, she greeted him enthusiastically, saying Leah was supposed to call and confirm she was arriving on Wednesday, but she must have forgotten.

"We don't have buggies here in Pinecraft and the minibus drops folks off about a mile and a half from where I'm staying. So before these old legs of mine hobble over there to collect her, I wanted to be sure she wasn't delayed again."

Jonathan was just about to tell Betty that Leah would actually be arriving in the main bus station instead, when Betty added, "Leah has said so many *wunderbaar* things about you, Jonathan. I'm looking forward to meeting you and I know Moses is relieved you'll be working with him, too."

Betty hardly took a breath as she continued to ramble, "After Leah had already missed so much of her vacation, I thought she was *narrish* for delaying her trip another full week after the blizzard instead of coming last Wednesday. But she's one stubborn *maedel* and she wanted to be sure everyone there was okay before she left. I'm *hallich* she's finally on her way and that you're coming, too."

Leah could have left right after the blizzard? She stayed in Fawn Crossing an extra week to make sure my familye *was okay? To make sure I was okay?*

Jonathan felt so ashamed that he couldn't tell Betty he wasn't coming or even that Leah would be on a different bus. He simply said goodbye and exited the phone shanty. Instead of getting back into the buggy, he ambled down the side of the road. Then he shuffled back, turned around and ambled down the road again.

I've really made a mess of things, he told himself. *How am I ever going to make this right?* His chest felt tight and his heart was racing. Even thought there was a stiff wind blowing, he broke out in a sweat. The buggy seemed so far away. His legs trembling, Jonathan knelt down and buried his head in his hands. *Please,* Gott, *give me a second chance with Leah. Please soften her heart toward me.*

Shortly after Leah had gone upstairs to her room, Nancy and Paul stopped in, just as they'd agreed to do every afternoon while Jonathan was away, in order to check on Esther and Gabriel and help them with whatever they needed. Leah was utterly humiliated to have to explain her change in plans, but as it turned out, Paul needed to go to the hardware store in town and he offered to take Leah with him so she could purchase a new ticket.

As Leah sat next to the deacon in his buggy on the return trip, she tried to make polite conversation, but she drew a blank. She should have felt relieved, since she'd reserved the last seat on the *Englisch* bus headed south from Fawn Crossing. The transportation company even gave her credit for the ticket on the minibus, which she wasn't expecting. But Leah couldn't overcome her feelings of disappointment. One week. Her vacation had been reduced from one month to one week and for what? A man who resented her for trying to help him,

"That looks like the Rockes' buggy," the deacon said, pointing in the direction of the phone shanty.

"Hmm," Leah murmured. *Jonathan must be calling Moses to disappoint him, too.*

About a quarter of a mile down the street, they noticed a round, dark object to the side of the road. Because it was nearly dusk, it was difficult to identify what they were looking at. "Did someone hit a deer?" Paul asked as they drew nearer.

"Absatz!" Leah demanded, recognizing the person's coat. "It's Jonathan!"

Every angry feeling she had toward him dissolved as she and Paul scrambled out of the carriage. *Please, Lord, let him be all right. Please, Lord,* Leah pleaded silently as she raced toward Jonathan, who was curled forward in a ball, clutching his stomach and rocking, as if in pain.

"Suh, are you hurt?" Paul asked, as he placed a hand on Jonathan's shoulder. Jonathan merely groaned, so Leah took charge.

"Jonathan," she said firmly, crouching beside him. "Look at me."

He lifted his head. His face was ruddy and the tears in his eyes were magnified by his glasses. He blinked, as if he couldn't believe it was her. "I'm so sorry, Leah." He made a choking sound and dropped his head again.

"Are you hurt?" the deacon repeated. "Do you need a *dokder*?"

"Neh—" Jonathan protested, but Leah interrupted him, asking the deacon to call the nurse practitioner and request that she come to the Rocke house.

Then she helped Jonathan back into his buggy and took the reins. As they journeyed, Jonathan apologized again. "You are the least selfish person I've ever known. And you were absolutely right. My bad mood has affected everyone else, especially you. I'm sorry."

"It's okay," Leah assured him. Seeing how broken he was made her realize she'd lost sight of the fact that he wasn't *choosing* to feel so low, and now that he'd apologized for insinuating she'd only been looking out for her own best interests, she forgave him.

The nurse practitioner arrived at the house a few minutes after Leah, Jonathan and the deacon did. Because she wanted privacy to consult with Jonathan alone, he met with her in his home while Paul went to assure the others that everything was going to be okay. Leah waited on Jonathan's porch, so nervous that she didn't even notice how cold it had gotten.

After about twenty minutes, the nurse practitioner opened the door and stepped outside. "Jonathan said I could tell you that I think he suffered a panic attack. I've made some recommendations and he's agreed to seek help if he experiences another attack or any other troublesome symptoms, but otherwise, I'm going to follow up with him in three weeks."

Leah thanked her and went inside, where she found Jonathan sitting at the table, drinking tea. He had a quilt draped over his shoulders and his hair was disheveled, which made him look particularly boyish, but he appeared much calmer now.

"The nurse practitioner said she thought you were right about me having seasonal affective disorder. She thinks that's partly why I was more vulnerable to experiencing a panic attack. I should have listened to you about getting help sooner. Leah, I'm so sorry for all I've put you through," he apologized for a third time.

"It's okay, I forgive you for the things you said. But I'm not the one who has been through a lot—you have. I know you don't want to feel as…as miserable as you've been feeling. And I admire how hard you've fought to keep going, despite how challenging it's been. I hope you'll forgive me for the mean things *I* said, too."

Jonathan nodded solemnly, holding her gaze. "Absolutely."

Leah took a deep breath and then hinted, "You know, it's not too late to go to Florida."

"You'd still want me to go with you?"

"Of course I would," Leah assured him. "But unfortunately, I bought the last ticket, so we can't go together. You can have mine though. I'll *kumme* on the next bus I can catch. Just don't cheat and practice shuffleboard on a real court without me!"

Jonathan cracked up, slapping the table. Leah didn't think her joke was that funny. "What's *voll schpass*?" she asked.

"I must have bought the next-to-the-last ticket right before you purchased yours!" he explained. "That's why I went back to town."

"You had decided to go to Florida after all?"

"*Neh*. The ticket wasn't for me, it was for you. I felt

so *baremlich* that I'd ruined your plans I decided the least I could do was spare you the extra expense of buying a regular bus ticket."

That is exactly the kind of considerate, lovely thing Jonathan has done for me time and again, and this time, he did it even though we were fighting, so it has *to be genuine.* Leah couldn't stop smiling.

"Don't you see?" Jonathan marveled. "It's not an accident that we purchased the last two tickets. It's as if the Lord is showing me in no uncertain terms that I ought to go with you…that I ought to *be* with you."

He got up and came around to Leah's side of the table. He took the quilt from his shoulders and wrapped it around hers, then knelt so his blue eyes were level with hers. "Leah, would you have me as your suitor?"

"Jah!" Leah exclaimed. "And I know the first place I'd like you to take me!"

Epilogue

"Eee!" Rebekah screamed, skittering backward across the sand, away from the breaking waves.

Esther, Gabriel, Leah and Jonathan all laughed as they watched the toddler's antics.

Moses Kasdorf was so impressed with Jonathan's workmanship the previous winter, he'd told him he could live in the bungalow free of charge for the month of December, provided he'd stay on and work through March. So Jonathan and Leah had come there for their honeymoon and they'd rented their own place for the next three months after that. But they were too lonely to spend Christmas alone, so they'd invited Esther, Gabriel and Rebekah to join them over the holidays.

"The water is colder than I thought it would be," Esther remarked.

"And the sand is a lot whiter than *I* thought it would be. It almost looks—I hate to say this—like *snow*," Gabriel said, laughing.

"I'm *hallich* it's not," Jonathan said.

"Me, too." Leah squeezed her husband's hand. As

she gazed out over the aqua water, she sighed. "I never get tired of looking at it."

"I hope you still feel that way when we *kumme* here again next winter," Jonathan said. The arrangement had been so beneficial for his health that he and Gabriel had agreed he should continue spending four months in Florida each year.

"I will—as long as we're together," Leah assured him before kissing his cheek. Then she whispered into his ear, "And who knows, by then we might even have a playmate for Rebekah…"

* * * * *

Look for a new Amish miniseries by Carrie Lighte, coming soon from Love Inspired Books!

Dear Reader:

I didn't realize how fortunate I was to grow up in New England, where we have four distinct seasons, until I moved to a place where there were essentially only two: "rainy" and summer—and the rainy season lasted disproportionately longer than the summer season! I felt similar to how Jonathan felt during my first year of living there. Suffice it to say, I coped by taking lots of naps and eating lots of comfort food. (If I had known about Pinecraft at that time, I would have scheduled a trip under the guise of "research" for my books.)

There's a quote from journalist Hal Borland that the Amish often use that goes, "No winter lasts forever. No spring skips its turn." Even though it sometimes seems that warmer, sunnier times are painfully slow in coming, I've found this saying to be true both literally and figuratively, haven't you?

Wherever you are as you're reading this right now, I hope you're experiencing the promise of spring and the presence of Christ.

Blessings,
Carrie Lighte

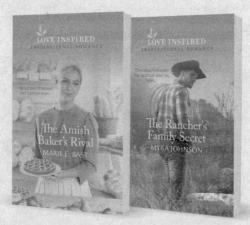

SPECIAL EXCERPT FROM

LOVE INSPIRED
INSPIRATIONAL ROMANCE

*Rescuing a single mom and her triplets during a
snowstorm lands rancher Finn Brightwood with
temporary tenants in his vacation rental. But with his
past experiences, Finn's reluctant to get too involved in
Ivy Darling's chaotic life. So why does he find himself
wishing this family would stick around for good?*

Read on for a sneak preview of
Choosing His Family, *the final book in*
Jill Lynn's Colorado Grooms *miniseries.*

In high school, Finn had dated a girl for about six months. Once,
when they'd been watching a movie, she'd fallen asleep tucked
against his arm. His arm had also fallen asleep. It had been a
painfully good place to be, and he hadn't moved even though he'd
suffered through the end of that movie.

This time it was three little monkeys who'd taken over his
personal space, and once again he was incredibly uncomfortable
and strangely content at the same time.

Reese, the most cautious of the three, had snuggled against
his side. She'd fallen asleep first, and her little features were so
peaceful that his grinch's heart had grown three sizes.

Lola had been trying to make it to the end of the movie, fighting
back heavy eyelids and extended yawns, but eventually she'd
conked out.

Sage was the only one still standing, though her fidgeting from
the back of the couch had lessened considerably.

Ivy returned from the bunkhouse. She'd taken a couple of trips
over with laundry as the movie finished and now returned the
basket to his laundry room. She walked into the living room as the
movie credits rolled and turned off the TV.